ADVENTURES OF SAMMY & WENDY

ADVENTURES OF SAMMY & WENDY

VOLUME I

R.K. BANDI

A Family Books Publisher
Virginia

First published in the United States 2018 by:
A Family Books Publisher
PO Box 147, Fairfax Station, VA 22039
www.afamilybooks.com

Text in this book is set in Book Antiqua

Printed in the United States of America

18 19 20 21 22 23 24 10 9 8 7 6 5 4 3 2 1

Publisher's Cataloging-in-Publication Data
Names: Bandi, R.K., author & cover designer. | McArdell, Alex, cover illustrator. | Bandi, D.K., Bandi, R.K., & Bandi, S., chapter illustrations. | Bandi, D.K., Bandi, N.K., Bandi, S., & Giasson, T., editors.
Title: Adventures of Sammy & Wendy / R.K. Bandi.
Description: First Edition. | Fairfax, Virginia : A Family Books Publisher, 2018.- | Series: Arrangement, v. I.- | Audience: 4 to 12. | Summary: "Sammy and Wendy, two middle graders, thwart bullies and embark on a series of extraordinary adventures."--Provided by publisher.
Identifiers: LCCN 2018902760 | ISBN 978-1-7320739-0-6 (hardcover)
Subjects: LCSH: Magic--Juvenile fiction. | Friendship in Children--Juvenile fiction. | CYAC: Adventure--Fiction. | Fantasy--Fiction. | Humor--Fiction. | Science--Fiction. | Bullies--Fiction. | LCGFT: Fantasy fiction. | BISAC: Juvenile Fiction / Action & Adventure / General.
Classification: LCC PZ7.1.B364Ad 2018. | DDC 823.92--dc23.

I. Bandi, RK. Auth. II. Title III. Series

DEDICATION

This book has been written especially for you. My hope is that you will read it to someone special to share the joys of living, learning, and loving, as I have done with my wonderful kids.

ACKNOWLEDGMENTS

I would like to thank my dear children for their unwavering dedication to editing and drawing the beautiful chapter illustrations for the adventures you are about to read. I want to thank my sister for her support and my generous friend that is also one of my editors for providing invaluable guidance. I am very grateful for my loving mother and friends who have profoundly influenced my life and personal character.

THE ADVENTURES

I. Mystical Minute Glass 1

II. Secret Monkey Kingdom 17

III. Enchanting Song Bird 29

IV. Defying Gravity 36

V. Outsmarting the Bullies 49

VI. The Times Machine 57

VII. Space Camp 69

VIII. Magic Beans 89

IX. Cloaking Cap 101

X. Interstellar Visit 115

I. Mystical Minute Glass

The origin of Old Greenwich, a small town immersed in lore, was mysterious even to the people who lived there. Local rumor had it that the lands were once home to a magical society, but the townsfolk were generally simple and didn't pay much attention to the unfounded legends...

It was finally the weekend, a chance for Sammy Flynn to sleep in late. Except when the morning arrived, he was disturbed by the sound of clanking pots from below. He managed to stretch open one eye as the sun's golden rays penetrated his bedroom window. Sammy typically slept on the floor with a sleeping bag because he preferred a harder surface. He tried to go back to sleep, but the smell of food cooking made his stomach rumble.

He forced himself up and stumbled towards the stairs. His sister, Wendy, enjoyed cooking breakfast and was already awake, helping their mother.

Sammy stepped into the kitchen, still tired. "Morning, everyone."

"Good morning! Did you sleep well last night?" asked Mrs. Flynn.

"Almost. I was dreaming about a quiet day at the beach when this flock of candy started flying by. I tried to catch one, but these horrible banging sounds scared them away."

"Oops! *Sorrry...* Did our cooking disturb you? Well, don't worry because my delicious blueberry pancakes won't fly away," teased Wendy.

"Awesome! I'm really hungry," he said, eyes widening. He poured himself some juice in a glass and sat at his favorite spot at the table, grabbing the warm syrup as Wendy passed him a steaming stack.

"Looks like you're extra hungry this morning," remarked Mr. Flynn, staring at the syrup in vain.

"Yep! Sorry about that, Pa. Wouldn't want my favorite pancakes getting cold," smiled Sammy, taking a big bite. "These are amazing!"

He was halfway through his scrumptious meal when a rather sweet blueberry gave him an idea. "You know what, Wendy? We should grow our own blueberry bush. Wanna go to the woods after eating?"

"Sure! I'll save some to take with us."

"Cool, and I'll get the shovel and my pocketknife!"

Sammy had a strong imagination and was always curious about his surroundings. Any reason to use his pocketknife was exciting, like the time he tried to whittle a long stick into a spear.

The Flynns lived in a traditional house surrounded by ancient woods that stretched for miles. It was the gently rolling hills, hidden caves, and a magnificent lake nearby that made their home special to the siblings.

They got ready and headed out the back door, taking the clearest path into the woods. They felt guarded by the trees. It was like being surrounded by an invincible army meant to protect them.

As they peered in the direction of the lake, they could see mist curling off the water in the distance. Wendy particularly enjoyed the gentle, morning breeze blowing through her reddish-brown hair. The smell of blooming flowers, maples, and dried pine needles permeated the air as they searched for a perfect spot to plant the blueberries.

Sammy looked around and found a bare patch of soil around the base of a huge oak tree where plenty of sunlight shone. He pulled out his shovel and stuck it in the ground. "I'll dig my way to China!" he joked.

Pushing the shovel deeper into the dirt, he heard a metal clank. "Did you hear that?"

"Yeah, what could it be?"

"I'm not sure." He carefully dug around it, exposing the corners of the unfamiliar object and could see the top of a small box emerge. "Maybe it's treasure!" he surmised.

Wendy reached down and gently pulled it out of the ground. It appeared to be very old and was lightweight. It was about the size of a jewel box. She rotated it, and could see fancy metal clasps and other fine designs engraved on it. She unlatched the clasps and slowly opened the lid. "It's an hour glass!" She carefully lifted the delicate glass object and handed it to Sammy.

It was about the size of his finger, fitting on the palm of his hand. "I think it's a minute glass." Examining it closely, he could see it did not have enough sand for an entire hour. Both ends of the cylindrical glass object were enclosed by two golden caps with unique engravings. "A master craftsman must have created this."

"Yeah, it's beautiful. Flip it over so we can see how long it takes for the sand to fall," said Wendy, hoping it would take a full hour.

"Okay, but I'm pretty sure I'm right," he said with confidence.

Sammy was about to flip it when he noticed a

small scroll in the box that Wendy held. "Hmm... I wonder what this is." He slowly unraveled the paper.

"Is there anything on it?"

"Yeah, I think so..." Sammy squinted at the faded writing. "'*The holder of this mystical glass can freeze all that is around upon reciting the following: This rhyme of mine will stop all time,*'" he read aloud as he flipped the finely crafted object.

Everything around him instantly froze. He had never seen Wendy so quiet before. She seemed even taller than before. Knowing his time was short, and that she might not believe him, he quickly carved a *W* on the oak tree with his pocketknife.

As the last grain of sand fell, everything began to move again. Wendy did not realize she had been standing there locked in time. Still peering at the glass, she said, "I wonder if anything will happen."

"Something *did* happen. A whole minute passed by. You didn't notice because you were frozen!"

"You're joking, right?"

"No, look... I carved that *W* on the tree," he pointed out.

She stared in amazement. "That's so cool!"

"Yeah, and I was right! It *is* a minute glass!" Glancing back at the scroll, he read the final line that said the magic would only work three times, so he only had two turns remaining. They returned home, excited about their discovery.

***

The next morning, they got ready and walked to the bus stop. Wendy's two best friends, Andrea Weaver and Lisa Banes, were happy to see her after their dull weekend. All three were in the eighth grade together.

The girls chatted about the latest gossip in school. "You won't believe it. I saw Abigail Hathaway and Ben Parker walking together in the hall," spilled Lisa. Abigail was the prettiest and most popular girl in school.

"Ben? Really? I thought he liked Deborah Gibbons?" asked Andrea, surprised at hearing the news. The girls began to giggle.

"So, tell me, Wendy... Which boy do you have your eye on these days?" asked Lisa with her ears perked.

"Well, you see, my eyes only have time for homework and projects." She was pretty enough, but she thought middle school boys were silly.

Sammy could see his best friend approaching. "Hey, Jason! How was your weekend?"

"Hey, Sammy, I didn't do anything too exciting, just homework and the usual chores."

"Same here. I tried searching for a stick to carve, but couldn't find a good one." He was about to tell

Jason about their discovery when he was distracted by Andrea's new hairstyle. "Uh, hi, Andrea, you look nice," Sammy stuttered.

"Thank you!" She smiled with part of her face hidden by her hair.

He thought she looked cute that way. She might not have been the most popular girl in school, but it was Andrea's personality and natural beauty that made Sammy's heart melt into his stomach.

Wendy and Lisa giggled after hearing him stumble his way through a compliment.

Jason poked him, suddenly jogging his daze. "Look who's coming," he said, frowning. They stared as three menacing troublemakers headed their way.

The leader of the trio was the infamous Bruteus "Brute" Baxter. He was big and brawny with a slightly round face. His hair was dark brown and spiky with a partial military style buzz on the sides. He cut the sleeves off from his black leather jacket to show off the knife tattoo he had on one arm and a skull on the other. Everyone knew he used markers to create them because he couldn't afford real ones.

He lived in a run-down trailer behind the abandoned steel factory. Rumor was that his old man lost his job when the factory shut down years ago, and his mama left when he was only five years old.

Ever since then, his father had to perform various odd jobs to raise him. He was a retired military man who kept a strict regimen that was hard for Brute to follow. He felt like a failure in the eyes of his father, so picking on other kids made him feel important.

He was supposed to be in high school, but was held back due to his low grades. Brute was not motivated by schoolwork. He even had to attend certain seventh grade classes, but no one dared to joke about it. His behavior earned him the reputation of being the biggest bully at school.

Next to him stood Zinfred Kort, nicknamed "The Zeek." He was a tall, lanky fellow with scruffy reddish hair, light freckles, and bit of an overbite. He usually wore the same grungy, beige t-shirt that said *Time to Rock and Roll* with a picture of Crazzy Mazzin's electric guitar on it. He was not very bright, always following whatever his friends did.

Then there was Maximillian Diggs who walked around with what looked like a permanent smirk. He preferred wearing pants rather than jeans and a black t-shirt with a red *Power Metal* logo. He just went by Max. He was smart, but avoided getting good grades to fit in with Brute and Zeek.

The three bullies made it to the curb just as the school bus approached. Brute stared everyone down as he and his buddies cut in front of the line. That was his way of signaling that no one else should get on the bus before them.

Mr. Alfonso, the bus driver, opened the door. He

had been driving the same bus since Sammy and Wendy were in elementary school. All the kids thought he was cool, except for the troublesome trio.

"Look at all these losers," sneered Zeek, attempting to step onto the bus first. All of a sudden, he felt a swift and heavy tug on his backpack followed by a smack to his head, which took him by surprise.

"Where you'z going? You know I gets on first," snarled Brute.

Zeek looked down to avoid provoking him even further. "Uh, yeah, sorry, Brute. I just got distracted in a moment of glory," squeaked Zeek.

Max followed them all the way to the back of the bus where they claimed sovereign territory. They liked to sit as far away from the bus driver as possible to hide their pranks. Mr. Alfonso didn't much like them. He waited until after they passed by before saying good morning to the other kids.

The bus was old, and the seats smelled like moldy vinyl. The back seats had pieces of duct tape that concealed some rips, courtesy of Brute and his sidekicks.

The road to school had the usual twists, turns, and bumps. All the kids began chanting, "Faster! Faster!" as the bus driver approached the best part of the ride.

Mr. Alfonso, in the spirit of the moment, sped up as the bus raced down the steepest hill. It felt just like a roller coaster to the kids. Even the troublemakers joined in for the thrill.

Their bus was the first to pull up in front of the school. The kids all stood up, anxious to depart. Brute and his gang took more time standing because they weren't excited about going to class.

"Enjoy your day," said Mr. Alfonso, waving as the other kids left. His cheery expression quickly vanished as the trio stepped off.

They lounged around outside waiting for everyone else to enter the school. All the other kids rushed in, wanting to stop at their lockers before the bell rang. Of course, the bullies had no concern about being on time for class.

Sammy enjoyed all of his classes, especially science and math. He was one of the smartest kids in the seventh grade.

His science teacher, Mr. Beeker, was nice, but at times absent-minded. Last week, for instance, he was going to hand out a pop-quiz, but Max distracted him with a question on how to achieve a self-sustaining fusion reaction. By the time Mr. Beeker finished explaining atomic theory, the bell had already rung.

For today's class, he set up stations for a lab assignment that required partners. Because of their misfit ways, Mr. Beeker wouldn't allow Max and Zeek to work together, so he paired Zeek with Sammy instead.

Sammy turned to Jason. "Look who I got stuck with..."

"Good luck, friend. I'm with Abigail! I think science is my favorite class now," smiled Jason.

"Yo, Sammy, just let me know when you're done, 'cause I'll be taking a snoozer," grinned Zeek.

Sammy wasn't happy about it, but arguing with him now would mean having to deal with his entire gang after class. While Zeek was dozing off, he quickly thought of an idea to teach him a lesson.

Sammy knew that Mr. Beeker required everyone to wash their hands at the end of each assignment, so he decided to shake some sulfur on the yellow soap to make it smell really bad.

Zeek stretched out his arms and yawned. "Well, looky here. Perfect timing. Hand over the lab results!" he demanded.

"Oh, I will, but class rules first. You have to wash your hands," reminded Sammy.

"Yeah, yeah, I'll do that." Zeek picked up the soap and rubbed it all over his hands. "What's that strange smell?" he asked, looking distressed.

"Oh, that's probably just the gas from the Bunsen burner." Sammy had to hold back his laughter to sound convincing.

At the end of class, Zeek walked out with Max as the odor lingered. Kids around him turned away.

Max suspected it was coming from Zeek but didn't want to embarrass him, knowing that he usually only showered once a week.

Brute approached Zeek's locker, cringing. "What's that horrible smells, Zeeko?"

"I don't know. Ever since I left science, I've been smelling it too," he said, waving his hand closer to Brute's face.

"Whoa! Don't waves your hands at me. It stinks!"

Max jumped in. "Yeah, I thought maybe you just didn't shower this morning."

"Haha, real funny, Max."

Suddenly, Zeek remembered smelling a bad odor after Sammy had told him to wash his hands at the end of the science lab. "Hey guys, I think Sammy messed with the soap I used. Let's go find him!" he shouted, yanking a shabby skateboard from his locker.

Max started to follow, decorating the lockers with a can of blue spray paint that he just found in the hall.

Brute was in no rush. He had been looking forward to eating the squished Twinkie in his pocket that he swiped earlier from some kid's lunch. He pulled it out and ripped off half the wrapper before taking a huge bite. "Alright, boys, I'm ready now. Let's pays a visit to your pal."

Ms. Smyte, their homeroom teacher, caught a

glimpse of the three hoodlums as they passed by her classroom.

Sammy was talking to Wendy when he saw trouble coming his way. He quickly pulled the minute glass out his backpack and stuck it in his pocket.

Zeek rolled up first. "Yo, Sammy, why do my hands smell like this?" he asked, shoving them close to Sammy's nose.

"Oh man! Maybe it's because you forgot to use toilet paper today?" Sammy swiftly turned his head, coughing, and covered his nose.

Wendy and her friends began to giggle seeing Zeek's angry expression.

"Why, I'll-" he started to respond, raising his hands.

Brute held him back. "Zeeko! Lets me handles the situations here... So, Sammy, buddy, I forgots my lunch money today, and I'm feelin' real hungry. How much you'z gots in your pockets there?" he asked, eyebrows scrunched.

"Well, hang on while I check." Sammy fished around in his pocket and slowly pulled out the minute glass.

"I'm not interested in no toys, just your money, so hands it over!" demanded Brute.

"Oh, this is no toy. *This rhyme of mine will stop all*

time!" cleverly recited Sammy as he flipped the mystical minute glass.

Everyone around him immediately froze. He quickly grabbed Brute's finger and placed it into Zeek's nose. He then lifted Zeek's finger into Max's nose. And to complete his masterpiece, he raised Max's finger into Brute's nose.

Sammy could see Ms. Smyte was trying to catch up to the troublemakers, so he gathered his books just before the last bit of sand dropped.

Time instantly resumed, but only one spell remained for the minute glass. All of the kids in the hallway broke down into hysterical laughter when they saw the bumbling cohorts with their fingers stuck in each other's noses.

"Nice work, Sammy! I know what you just did." Wendy winked.

Ms. Smyte saw the horrible scene just before Brute pushed Max, Max pushed Zeek, and Zeek smacked himself, falling back on the lockers.

"Max, what was you'z thinking puttin' your fingers in my nose?" angrily asked Brute.

"Uh... Uh... I didn't put it there! Zeek, why did *you* stick your finger in my nose?" asked Max, shuddering at the bad smell still lodged in there.

"How should I know? Why did Brute have his finger in *my* nose?"

"Alright, boys! That's enough horseplay! I want the three of you to follow me to the principal's office, right now!" ordered Ms. Smyte.

Not getting the chance to place blame on Sammy for his smelly hands, Zeek gave him the evil eye as they marched away.

The teacher did her best to explain the terrible things she had seen to Principal Weinheimer. "These young men have a problem pointing their fingers where they shouldn't be."

"Thank you, Ms. Smyte. I'll take it from here." She gladly returned to her class. "I'd like you boys to stick around, if you know what I mean."

"Uh, you seez, we'z just talking to our friends in the hall, and for some reason, our fingers got stucks into each other's noses," sheepishly explained Brute with little success.

"Well, boys, it sounds a bit fishy to me, and you take the saying 'pointing is rude' to a whole new level. Plan on being my guests in detention for the rest of this week!"

They were really frustrated because there was nothing further they could say to justify their previously precarious postures.

When school finally ended, Sammy, Wendy, and their friends boarded the bus in peace for once. Even Mr. Alfonso was relieved that the troublemakers were in detention. The kids cheered, knowing the bus ride would be bully-free for the rest of the week.

That evening, Sammy's mother prepared a special veggie-ball pasta with garlic bread and a salad for dinner. They enjoyed family meals because it gave them a chance to talk about the day's events.

Sammy told his father about Zeek not doing any work for the lab assignment, and the peculiar events that followed.

"Well, I hope he learned a good lesson about doing his own work from now on, and not '*picking*' on others," chuckled Mr. Flynn.

"Oh, I'm sure he did," giggled Wendy.

After finishing dinner and their homework, the siblings prepared for bed. Mrs. Flynn tucked them in. "Good night, Sammy. Goodnight, Wendy. And sweet dreams...," she whispered, turning off the lights.

II. Secret Monkey Kingdom

It was winter break, and the Flynns had planned a trip to South America. They chose to visit the Amazon rainforest because they preferred to take a vacation in a warm climate. It would be their first time leaving the country.

That night, the siblings were busy preparing for the trip. Sammy packed his compass, binoculars, flashlight, and of course, his pocketknife. Wendy packed her favorite stuffed animal, hairbrush, and a few games so they wouldn't get bored. They had to be up early, so they put everything away and fell asleep.

It felt like only a few minutes had passed when

Mrs. Flynn yelled from the bottom of the stairs. "Sammmy... Wennndy.... Wake up! Time to get ready!"

Sammy didn't feel like opening his eyes, but he didn't have a choice. Peeking from his sleeping bag, he could see Wendy's hand hanging off his bunk bed. She liked camping in his room whenever he agreed. He didn't mind because they usually played games before going to sleep. He reached over and tugged on her blanket. "Wendy, are you awake?"

She grunted and pulled her blanket back over her head. "I am now," she muttered, stretching her arms.

"Today's the day!"

"Yeah, I heard Mama calling," she said, dragging herself out of bed, eyes still half closed.

After washing up, they raced down the stairs.

Wendy was the first to reach the kitchen. "Good Morning!" she said with a smile.

"Are you two set for the big trip?" asked Mr. Flynn.

"We sure are!" she excitedly replied.

"Morning, Pa! What's the name of that city we're going to visit?" asked Sammy.

"It's called Guadalana. It's a small village near the Amazon river."

After enjoying their wonderful breakfast, Mr. Flynn packed their bags into the car. He was great at organizing the trunk. "Everyone ready? On to the airport!"

The drive to the airport was nice. Once inside the terminal, Sammy and Wendy could see gigantic airplanes through the window, including the one they would be flying on.

When it was time to board, they handed their tickets to the flight attendant. Their parents followed.

The pilot welcomed everyone aboard with a big smile. After finding their row, Sammy rushed to take the window seat.

"Hey, I wanted to sit there!" whined Wendy. She wanted to see what was happening outside the plane.

"Sorry, beat you to it."

The pilot announced they were about to depart, so everyone had to buckle their safety belts. Sammy imagined he was on a spaceship ready to take off.

The plane approached the runway. With a sudden pull, it accelerated far faster than the Flynns had ever experienced. As the plane lifted off, their stomachs felt a little funny.

"Wow, this is really cool!" shouted Wendy as she felt the g-force.

"Yeah, it feels like a swing!" responded Sammy.

Everything on the ground below looked small as he peered out the window. Cars, trucks, and even houses looked like toys. It was going to be a long journey, so he was glad Wendy brought some games that they could play. Their parents slowly nodded off into a deep sleep.

The following morning, they landed at Manuas International Airport. They collected their bags and waited for their ride. It was hot and humid outside, and they could hear the sounds of wild birds all around.

An old bus pulled up to take them to their destination. It was painted with many bright colors. Mr. Flynn had reserved a traditional jungle hut located deep in the rainforest. The kids stared out the window as they moved along, taking in the tropical scenery of the rainforest.

The bus stopped at the central station. A local driver with a rusty, open-air Jeep greeted them. It was the only vehicle available that could navigate the mountainous terrain.

Sammy and Wendy really enjoyed the wind blowing in their faces as they traveled through the mountains over steep bumpy roads. They could see the area where they would be staying as it appeared around the bend of the mountain.

The walls of the hut were constructed from mud and straw, and the roof was made from bamboo intertwined with banana leaves. An array of tropical plants and trees surrounded the area. They jumped out of the Jeep and the driver helped carry their bags.

With a swift jerk, Sammy swung open the front door. He pretended to be a cowboy entering a bar in the Wild West. It was strangely cool inside compared to the hot, tropical air outside.

The driver explained that the breeze blowing through the moist leaves on the roof created a natural air conditioner, keeping the hut cool on the inside. Just before leaving, he warned, "Do not go beyond the river without a guide. You will get lost. Also, be aware that ancient spirits roam the rainforest. It's not good to disturb them."

"Spirits? What do you mean?" asked Wendy.

"Well, according to local myth, there was once a flourishing civilization that was destroyed thousands of years ago, but their treasures remain hidden in the jungle. It is said that the spirits are from the people of that long forgotten nation, still wanting to protect their land," replied the driver as he left.

Sammy was intrigued by the driver's story. "Pa, can we go exploring?"

"It's been a long journey. How about you two look around while your mother and I rest, but don't go too far," instructed Mr. Flynn.

"Sure, Pa!"

Sammy grabbed his backpack, and they headed out. "Wendy, there's another hut on that hill over there." He looked through his binoculars. "I think it's empty. Let's check it out." They walked up to it.

The front door was open. They could see rays of sunlight peering through the roof. There were used dishes with dried stains on the table. "Looks like it has been abandoned for a while," commented Wendy.

"Hmm... I wonder what this paper is." Sammy held it up to the sunlight. He could see a path was drawn to an area marked with an *X* just beyond a river. "It looks like a map!"

"Let me see! I love a great mystery."

"Wanna follow it?" he asked.

"Well, I'm kind of feeling tired now, so maybe we can go tomorrow."

Sammy agreed and they headed back to their hut.

Mrs. Flynn was happy they had returned. "Hope you two enjoyed your exploration. "I prepared a special meal for the evening, so wash up."

"Oh, really? What did you make?" asked Wendy.

"I used a century old native recipe to make plantain stew and mashed yams with maize tortillas."

"Planting stew?" asked Sammy, frowning.

"Mashed yams with amazing tortillas?" asked Wendy, not knowing if she had heard it right the first time.

"It's *plantain* stew and *maize* tortillas, but don't worry, I'm sure you'll love it," replied Mrs. Flynn.

The food tasted pretty good to them even though they didn't want to let on about it.

With their bellies full, the siblings could hardly keep their eyes open. Heavy rain started beating down on the roof. They crawled into their sleeping bags and quickly fell into a dreamy slumber.

Early in the morning, Mr. Flynn wanted to wake them up, but as he entered their room, a loud screeching sound came from outside.

Wendy awoke, startled by the noise. "What was that?"

"Oh, probably a jungle animal waking up its family," said Mr. Flynn, voice raised, hoping Sammy would wake up.

"Uh, good morning, Pa," he mumbled, struggling to open his eyes.

"Good morning, Sammy. Hope you were comfortable last night. Mama made some tasty breakfast."

"Oh, good, 'cause I'm real hungry," he said, stomach rumbling. Wendy was also extra hungry being in a new environment.

"Morning, Mama. What's for breakfast? I'm starving!" asked Sammy, entering the kitchen.

"Oh, I made grilled grain bread with mango jelly. You can also try this local wheat cereal with some fresh coconut milk."

"Aww, Mama! Didn't you bring our Koco Krunchers?" Wendy whined.

"No dear, it's good to try new things."

They tried the food, but it didn't really compare to hot hash browns and waffles with warm syrup back home.

After breakfast, they brushed their teeth using a native black powder on a twig. It felt like a huge toothpick with sand in their mouths, but it sure cleaned their teeth well.

Their parents decided to spend the morning relaxing in a mud bath. Sammy was slow to finish his breakfast.

"Come on, Sammy. Grab the map and your backpack, and let's go!" shouted Wendy, impatiently tapping her foot.

"Pa, we're heading out. Hope you enjoy your dirt bath," snickered Sammy.

"It's *mud,* not dirt. Remember not to go past the river, and come back before lunch."

"Okay, bye!"

They bolted out the door, anxious to know where the map would lead them. Sammy used his compass to help navigate the vast rainforest. He could see a large banana tree ahead of him and just *had* to climb it.

Wendy watched as he struggled to move through the massive leaves. "You're a real monkey, but be careful!"

"Uh, I'm almost there. I think I can reach them..." He pulled a bundle of bananas and carefully climbed back down. He detached two and gave one to Wendy before putting the rest in his backpack.

Walking towards the river, they slowly peeled the delicious fruit. Wendy almost took a bite of hers when some type of animal suddenly swung down from a tree, snatched it from her hand, and landed on another tree. She turned around and saw a cute monkey with a long tail staring down at her.

"Hey! That's mine! Give it back!"

The monkey just smirked before grabbing a vine and swinging across a narrow part of the river to the other side. It looked back across the rushing water, dangling upside down from a branch with the yellow fruit still in its hand.

"Let's go after him!" yelled Wendy, determined to catch up with the escaping thief. Without thinking about the driver's warning, she ran to the edge of the bank, grabbed the nearest vine, and swung across too. The monkey was surprised, but also amused.

"Come on, Sammy!" she shouted from the other side.

He was not as strong a climber as she was, but he managed to swing across without any problem.

They rushed up the hill to catch up with the monkey. Sammy noticed a ghostly looking tree with multiple arms reaching out. He remembered seeing it drawn on the map that he was carrying. "Wendy, I think we're on the right path."

Recalling the driver's story, she began to worry. "Okay, but remember what the driver told us about not crossing the river? Maybe we should turn back before we disturb the wandering spirits."

"Oh, I'll just leave a couple of bananas at this tree just in case the spirits are hungry. That should keep them busy," replied Sammy.

The cute monkey suddenly reappeared, still licking its lips from finishing the stolen fruit. This time, however, it was wearing some ancient head covering. It reached down and grabbed the banana that Sammy left at the tree and signaled for them to follow.

The siblings were surprised, but they had a feeling the monkey was friendly, so they agreed to go.

They hiked deeper into the jungle until they approached a hidden cave entrance wreathed with vines and huge red flowers.

Sammy pulled a flashlight from his bag and led the way through the cave's winding tunnels.

Eventually, the passageway opened into a large cavern with images all over the walls. The paintings showed an ancient civilization where monkeys and humans lived together, helping each other survive. One image showed them fighting in a great battle against invaders.

As they stood in awe, a large monkey wearing a jeweled headband and golden armor slowly approached. Following behind it were many other monkeys that remained respectfully quiet. The cute monkey walked up to the leader to give him the banana from the ghostly tree.

"Many before you have come in search of our treasure!" exclaimed the leader monkey, glaring at the siblings.

They were shocked to hear it speak. "I'm Sammy, and this is my sister, Wendy. We come in peace." He always wanted to say that line. "How is it that you can speak?" he asked.

"We are descendants from a long line of guards that served Atahualpa in the ancient city of Teocajhas. He was a great king who taught us how to speak."

"Who were the invaders drawn on the wall?" asked Wendy.

"They were the Spanish conquistadors. When they attacked, the King entrusted my ancestors with the sacred scrolls of knowledge. They contain the history of our civilization and a map to the kingdom's treasure."

"A map? Is this it?" asked Sammy, pulling out the tattered paper from his pocket.

The leader looked at it. "No, this map only leads to our caves. We hid the scrolls deep in the rain forest where no human could ever find them. Our guards will scare away anyone that crosses the river to protect them."

"Oh, so they must be the wandering spirits. *Now* I understand," commented Wendy.

The leader's proud expression softened after hearing the cute monkey chatter and point to the humans. "My young guard just told me that you have honored our sacred tree with fruit of the jungle. For this good deed, I shall reward you both. I only ask that you keep our existence a secret. The treasure must remain protected until the rightful heir returns, as the prophecy has foretold!"

"Yes, sir, we promise," they said.

The leader handed Wendy a shimmering bracelet with rubies and emeralds, and gave Sammy a heavy bag of ancient gold coins. With big smiles, they said thank you and waved goodbye before traveling back to their hut.

"Mama! Pa! Look at my beautiful bracelet!" rejoiced Wendy.

"And my bag of gold coins!" added Sammy.

Their parents, still cleaning the mud from their faces, couldn't really see too well. They smiled and assumed the two were just joking.

The family had a great time in the Amazon, but they were ready to return home. It was a long flight, so they leaned back, covered themselves with cozy blankets, and fell into a deep and relaxing sleep.

III. Enchanting Song Bird

One fine Sunday morning, the siblings were in the woods behind their house, searching for different types of leaves for Wendy's science project.

Sammy was starting to get bored. "Wanna play hide and seek like we used to?"

"Sure! I have enough leaves now, so you hide, and I'll count!" She was excited because it had been a long time since they played that game. She stood behind a large oak tree and covered her eyes. Raising her voice, she began to count, "One... Two... Three..."

He darted around the woods looking for a good spot to hide and managed to wiggle his way behind a tall bush. He squatted down to stay hidden.

"Nine... Ten! Ready or not, here I come..." Wendy started searching for him, running from tree to tree.

Sammy heard a rustle in the bush that he was hiding behind. He looked up and could see that a very small, colorful bird was stuck between the twigs. He immediately stood up and signaled for Wendy to come quietly.

He whispered, "There's a bird stuck in this bush. I think it might be injured."

The bird sang a sad song. Sammy reached in and slowly moved the twigs away from its body. "Hi, Birdie. So sorry you got stuck." He gently cupped the fragile bird between his palms. He could see another small twig tied around its feet and removed that too.

It had the brightest mix of blue, yellow, green, and red colors that he had ever seen. Sammy made sure the bird was okay before completely opening his hands.

It raised its head high, flapped its wings, and then flew into the air. It sang a happy tune as it flew away. To Sammy, it sounded exactly like,

"*Thank you so much. My life you spare, and one day you need me, I'll be there.*"

"Wow, that was an amazing bird," Wendy remarked.

"I'm just glad it's okay. Did you hear that?" he asked.

"Yeah, it sounded beautiful," she said, not realizing that Sammy had actually heard words.

They returned home excited to have helped the songbird. "Mama! Mama! We found this really beautiful bird that was stuck in a bush and Sammy saved it," panted Wendy.

"That's so nice, Sammy. Did you both clean your rooms?" Mrs. Flynn asked.

"We're on it!" They quickly raced upstairs before she could suggest any other chores.

After cleaning, they spent the rest of the evening finishing their homework. History reading was especially tiring, so they fell asleep early.

The next day in the school cafeteria, Sammy sat with his friends; Jason, Brandon, and Jeffrey. They enjoyed playing cards everyday at lunch.

Brandon had a great sense of humor. He loved to joke around, but he was a good kid. Jeffrey was fairly strong, but never used his strength to hurt anyone.

Wendy sat with Lisa, Andrea, and Deborah. They enjoyed talking about homework, boys, and other gossip.

Sammy was busy talking to Jeffrey when Brandon looked towards the lunch line. "Looks like Brute and his gang are up to no good again. Zeek is swiping burgers and passing them back to Brute and Max."

"Oh, boy. One day they're seriously going to get

caught," commented Jeffrey.

"Maybe, but the lunch lady is way too slow and focused on collecting money to notice what those guys are doing," remarked Sammy.

The cafeteria was extra crowded today because the sixth graders had a combined lunch with them. Unfortunately, the only spaces left were at Sammy's table. He and his friends tried not to make eye contact with the bullies, hoping they would just pass them by.

Max was observant and looked around for empty seats. "Hey, Brute. Looks like we'll have to take over Sammy's table today."

Brute was always looking to show off his strength. "Moves over! This is our tables now, so if you wants to stay, you gots to pay! Hands over them desserts!" he commanded.

"Uh, we were here first," stammered Sammy, attempting to rebel.

"Oh yeah? Well, it looks like you won'ts be needing them Twinkies, so better thanks me for taking it offs your hand!" growled Brute as he reached over and swiped it from him.

Jason, Brandon, and Jeffrey reluctantly passed their desserts to Max and Zeek to avoid further trouble.

Out of the corner of his eye, Sammy saw something small and colorful just outside one of the windows. It was the songbird looking at him.

After finishing lunch, the kids went outside for recess. Sammy looked around for the bird but couldn't find it, so he decided to play cards with his friends on a bench.

Brute and his buddies spotted them and wanted to stir up some more trouble. "Yo, Samster-the-hamster! I heard you'z was good at jumping. So lemme see ya jumps over this bench," he egged on.

Sammy thought the bench was too high for him and didn't want to get hurt. "Not interested," he sternly replied.

"If you'z refuse, you'z all gonna be sittin' on the floors during lunch for the rest of the weeks and paying us more tolls!"

Sammy didn't want trouble for his friends, so he thought he would give it a try.

The songbird was watching from a distance. Sammy walked back ten yards from the bench. The bird knew that he would not be able to clear it.

Sammy began to run. Just before he jumped, the enchanting songbird swooped down and cast a spell with a magic chirp that sounded like,

"For this boy in certain mire, let him rise, at least one foot higher."

Amazingly, Sammy cleared the bench and landed on his feet. His friends were shocked. Even Brute and his crew were surprised.

"No one, I says no one, jumps highers than me!" exclaimed Brute.

"Yeah, show them who's boss!" shouted Max.

Brute turned and walked ten yards back from the bench. A crowd of other kids began to gather. He carefully eyed his target and began to sprint towards it. He jumped with all his strength, but the songbird swooped down, casting another spell,

"*Boy of trouble, turn your pants to rubble!*"

Even though Brute cleared the bench, he tore the back of his jeans and stumbled while landing.

He was embarrassed about falling, but didn't realize his pants had ripped from behind. As soon as he opened his mouth to say some bad words, his voice squealed a tune,

"*Sing me a love song, sing it like a bird song…*"

Everyone heard and began to laugh. The songbird flew past Sammy and quietly tweeted to him,

"*Hope you had fun, my deed is done. Enjoy the rest of your day, it's my time to fly away...*"

Sammy understood and waved thanks to the bird while everyone else's attention was on Brute.

Max and Zeek were shocked. "Didn't know you could sing a pretty song, Brute," complimented Zeek with warm sincerity.

Brute smacked him upside his head. Before he

attempted to speak again, Ms. Brumbreaker, the cafeteria monitor, saw what had happened. She was a huge woman with broad shoulders and towered over all the other teachers. She never smiled to anyone and was always very strict. Rumor was that she was once a professional wrestler. Even Brute and his gang didn't dare cross her. "Bruteus Baxter! Jumping over school property is dangerous! March to the Principal's office, NOW!" she ordered.

Principal Weinheimer was very disappointed to see him again. "Bruteus, what, pray tell, is the reason you're honoring me with your presence again? And *please,* with all mercy, tell me why you're parading around with the back of your pants torn??"

Brute wanted to explain, but the only sounds that poured out of his mouth were,

"*Sing me a love song, sing it like a bird song…*"

"Well, if this is just a joke to you, then tell me how funny does three days of suspension sound?"

Daring not to reply again, Brute just nodded and gallantly accepted his punishment.

Max and Zeek didn't want to take any more chances after what happened to Brute, so they thought it would be best to leave Sammy and his friends alone. At least for a while...

IV. Defying Gravity

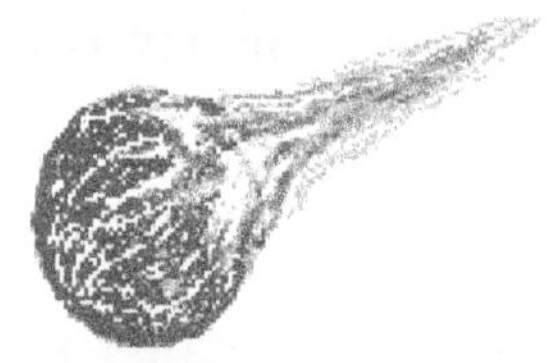

Sammy was relaxing and listening to the science station on the radio in his room one Friday evening. The spokesperson mentioned that Jupiter, Saturn, and Neptune could be seen at night with a telescope. He went on to explain that the three planets only aligned in the solar system once every thousand years.

Sammy was excited because he had the chance to see a rare event with his new telescope that he got for Christmas. "Hey, Wendy, wanna stay up late tonight to see some planets up close?"

"I'll try, but I might not be able to stay awake too late. You know how sleepy I get after homework."

Later that night, they climbed up their loft stairs to the highest window in their home. It was dark outside and the night sky was clear. They had never seen the stars so bright.

Sammy set up his telescope and peeked through the lens with one eye. He shifted it around and searched for Jupiter since it was the closest planet of the three.

"What do you see?" asked Wendy with a yawn, her eyes getting heavy.

"I think... Just a second." He adjusted the focus. "I do see something larger than a star. I think it's Jupiter! Cool! I can even see the other two planets. Come take a look at Saturn's rings!"

She peeked into the lens and could see the planets. "This is really neat. They're all in a line. Wait, didn't you say there were only three planets? I see a fourth one moving towards us!"

He quickly peered into the telescope. "You're right! It's bright and getting bigger!" The object got so large that Sammy could no longer see anything through his telescope.

"Look up there! I see something!" shouted Wendy, her eyes fixated on the night sky.

Sammy looked through the window and could see a huge ball of fire with a burning tail heading towards the lake. They watched as it crashed into the hillside, throwing a huge cloud of smoke and dirt in the air.

"Whoa! Did you see that? We have to check it out tomorrow morning!" They had never seen anything like that before. It was hard for Sammy to fall asleep with his mind fully charged, but eventually he settled down.

The next morning, sunlight seeped through the shades onto Sammy's face. He turned over to block the light and suddenly remembered it was time to search for the fallen orb. "Wendy, wake up! We have to go!"

"Huh? Uh, okay," she murmured.

After brushing their teeth, they headed down for breakfast. "Morning, Mama!" they said.

"Good morning, kiddos. How was the view from your telescope last night, Sammy?"

"Amazing! We saw Jupiter, Saturn, and Neptune. Then something else fell out of the sky. We're going out to find it." Sammy gobbled down his food.

"Sounds interesting, but please be careful," requested Mrs. Flynn, knowing he could get carried away with his imagination.

Sammy grabbed his backpack and they rushed out into the woods. They ran past familiar trees, shrubs, and fallen logs on their way to the lake.

The wind was calm, allowing the dragonflies to dance just above the water's surface. They walked around the lake and scoped out the hillside.

Sammy noticed the smell of burnt leaves in the air. "I see smoke rising over there. We must be close."

She peered in the same direction and saw a faint

stream of gray in the distance. They ran to the top of the hill. "Look, down there!" she shouted, pointing to a crater in the ground.

They made their way down the other side, but were careful in approaching the smoldering crash site. There, in the center of it all, lay a dark, porous rock about the size of a bowling ball, which was infused with chunks of metal. It left a scorched trail that stretched from the top of the hill to the crater.

"It's a meteorite!" exclaimed Sammy.

"Be careful, it might still be hot. You'd better not touch it," warned Wendy.

He picked up a stick and poked it, but nothing unusual happened. He quickly tapped it with his finger. "It's not hot anymore and seems to be harmless. I'm going to put it in my bag." He picked it up and realized it was not very heavy either.

Wendy offered to carry his bag. They headed back to the lake. "Let's wash the soot off our hands," she suggested.

"Great idea."

Once they reached the water, Wendy put the bag down and started to rinse her hands.

Sammy also dunked his hands. "Can you please grab me some napkins?" he asked politely.

She went back to open the bag and a small bit of water dripped off her finger onto the meteorite. The bag slowly began to rise. "Uh, Sammy, what's going on?"

He quickly reached up and grabbed it before it could fly away. "I don't know."

"I think the water from my hand caused the meteorite to float."

"Really? We'll have to test it again at home," he suggested.

They started walking back. After about five minutes, the meteorite had dried. The bag was no longer floating.

Later that evening, Sammy's mind began to wander while doing his homework. He started to think about how they could test the meteorite when an exciting idea popped into his mind. "Wendy, we're going to build an anti-gravity machine tomorrow, but we'll need supplies."

Wendy was deep in concentration trying to solve her math equations. "Uh huh, sure, Sammy... An anti- what?"

"An anti-gravity machine! You know, a device that can defy gravity. I'm going to draw up some plans for it right now!" He immediately pushed his homework aside and pulled out a fresh sheet of paper and started sketching.

"Good luck with that. I'm going to sleep!"

Sammy worked on his design until he couldn't

keep his eyes open any longer. That night, he tossed and turned in his sleeping bag, dreaming of possible ways to build the machine.

The next morning, he woke up to the sound of his father chopping wood in the back yard. He thought his sister was still asleep, so he quietly got up and grabbed his favorite jeans and a pair of torn socks.

Wendy heard him rustling around in his closet. "Don't make so much noise. I'm trying to sleep!" she shouted. Eventually, she got up too and headed downstairs with Sammy.

"Morning, Mama! Wendy and I are going to build an anti-gravity machine today!"

"Good morning. An anti- what machine?" replied Mrs. Flynn, seemingly confused.

"Yep, I said the same thing last night. He's planning to build a machine that can float!" Wendy added excitedly.

"Oh, I see... Looks like his imagination is flying high," giggled Mrs. Flynn.

After breakfast, Sammy and Wendy ran out back to gather supplies. "Morning, Pa! Can we use some of your wood for our project?"

"Good morning, kiddos! Sure. I have plenty for the fireplace, so have at it."

"Thanks, Pa!" shouted Sammy as he grabbed a stack. Wendy gathered some other supplies in the meantime.

They carried everything to their large shed, which looked like a miniature house. It was equipped with all sorts of tools and an old wooden pallet that was nearly four feet in width and six feet in length.

They began to build a wooden box on the pallet that was large enough to fit the meteorite. Sammy surrounded the space rock with brackets and chained it to the box. He also constructed a makeshift rudder to control the direction of the machine.

Wendy bolted two chairs to the platform and hung a shower curtain on a broomstick to act as a sail. When they were satisfied the machine was built according to Sammy's design, they dragged it outside. It was big enough for both of them to sit on.

Wendy held the water dropper while Sammy picked up the string that was attached to the rudder. "The wind will determine our speed and I'll steer."

"It looks awesome! I can't wait to try it out!"

They sat on the chairs. "Okay, we're ready to go, so put a little bit of water on it," instructed Sammy.

She squeezed and a single drop fell onto the meteorite, causing it to strain against the chains as it rose. They slowly gained altitude as the rock pulled up the entire machine, eventually reaching the top of their house.

"Should I raise the sail now?" asked Wendy.

"Yep, and I'll keep us from hitting the trees!"

"Let's fly to the park!" she suggested.

"Great idea! Five degrees starboard we go!" The light breeze gently pushed them as they flew over the lake.

Five minutes had passed since Wendy had added the first drop of water, and as the meteorite began to dry, they slowly descended on the park. They could see kids but they were too busy playing to notice that the siblings had just landed.

Wendy stepped off and a young girl about the age of four tugged her shirt from behind. "My baby kitten, Sniffles, is stuck up there. Can you please get her down for me?" she pleaded, pointing to a tall maple tree.

"Awww, sure, we can help you. Just stand back, and we'll get her," Wendy proudly responded.

Sammy was still sitting on his chair. "Add a half drop of water onto the meteorite and give the rope some slack while I float up, then grab it when I give you the signal," he instructed.

Wendy lightly squeezed the dropper, allowing a tiny amount of water to fall on the stone. The machine began to rise. The little girl's eyes opened wide, staring in wonder as she saw the machine float.

When Sammy gave the signal, Wendy held onto the rope as he gently coaxed the kitten to come down from the branch. "I got her, so you can pull me down now!"

Wendy pulled the rope until he reached the ground. "Here you go, little girl. Make sure your kitten stays home and doesn't climb up anymore trees," Sammy kindly told her.

"I will. Thank you for saving Sniffles. I can't wait to tell my mommy you can fly!" shouted the little girl as she ran home.

Wendy rolled the rope and hopped back onto the machine. She released another drop of water and they lifted off again.

Meanwhile, the three troublemakers were on their way to the park. "Hey, Brute, what's that up there?" asked Max, pointing to the craft.

"Hmm... Ain't never seen nothin' like thats before," he replied, peering at it in confusion.

"Maybe it's some sort of new kite," proudly added Zeek.

Brute knocked him upside his head in frustration. "Zeeko, ain't no kites that big. Do you seez anyone holdin' any strings down here?"

Zeek looked around. "Uh, I guess not. Was someone on it?"

"Yeah, it sure looked a lot like the Flynns to me. Maybe we should take a visit to their house," Max slyly suggested.

"Sure thing, but let's waits until it's darks around

ten tonight. We can meet ups at the bus stop," said Brute.

"Sounds like a plan!" responded Max.

"Yeah, and I'll wear my new sunglasses as a disguise," Zeek chimed in as he kicked a dent into the metal trashcan at the park.

Brute and Max stared at each other, frustrated that Zeek didn't realize that his sunglasses wouldn't really help him at night. They hung around to shoot hoops at the park before heading back to their homes.

Sammy and Wendy were still enjoying the incredible experience of flying. "The lake looks really cool from up here!" shouted Wendy, admiring the reflections and fresh breeze as they floated over the water.

"Yeah, it's really cool, but we need to head back before someone sees us," remarked Sammy, wishing they could fly a little longer.

Their father saw them just after they landed safely in the yard. "What's that machine you two built?"

"Hi, Pa! We built an anti-gravity machine using this meteorite we found yesterday. It floats when you put some water on it," explained Sammy.

Mr. Flynn assumed he meant it could float on water. "I see. I'm very proud that both of you used your creative skills and imagination to build it. Mama has lunch ready, so better wash up."

In all the excitement, they forgot how hungry they were and looked forward to the nice meal.

Sammy and Wendy told their mother about the kitten they saved at the park, but decided not to mention that the machine could fly. They couldn't wait to try it out again the next day. They were really tired that night and fell asleep early.

It was just after ten when the troublemakers met at the bus stop. They headed towards Sammy's house, discussing what they would do if they found the contraption.

They reached the Flynns' house and snuck around to the back where they could see the machine sitting under a large oak tree.

"Man, what is this thing? It looks cool! Can we please fly it to the top of the school?" pleaded Zeek.

"Let's move it first, just in case Sammy's parents are still up," suggested Max.

"Good ideas, Max. Grabs a corner Zeeko, and let's get this thing downs to the lake!" demanded Brute.

They quietly carried the unwieldy machine through the woods. They couldn't see very well in the dark, bumping into trees and stumbling over fallen branches along the way. The moonlight glimmered off the lake, helping guide them to it.

They set the contraption down. "Alright, Max, you knows about machines, so how do we'z fly this thing?" eagerly asked Brute.

Max didn't really know right away. He didn't want to disappoint the guys, so he carefully looked it over and tinkered with the various parts. Since it was made of wood and had a sail, he assumed it would float. "Guys, let's put it on the water. Maybe the wind will lift us up." They dragged the machine onto the water and quickly hopped aboard.

"Since we ain't got no paddles, why don't you'z two gets down and paddle us aways from the shore while I steer," commanded Brute, feeling like a pirate.

Zeek and Max bent down and began to slap the water, but they were hardly moving. "Put some more strength into it, Zeek!" Max ordered.

Zeek began to slap the water harder and suddenly a huge splash of water hit the meteorite. Almost immediately, it shot up into the air, knocking the three hooligans off the machine and straight into the lake. "Ahh! I can't swim! I can't swim!" shouted Zeek.

Brute smacked him upside his head with his wet hand. "Zeeko, we're in shallow waters. Just stands up and walks!"

"Uh, oh, right! Yeah, I knew that. Just joking!" he pretended.

The meteorite on the anti-gravity machine was soaked. It rose up so fast that it went straight back into space.

The three of them were very disappointed. It was

like they were watching a brand new birthday balloon fly away. Their clothes were drenched, so they returned home, cold and miserable.

The next morning, Sammy and Wendy were sad to see that their invention had disappeared. Sammy thought it might have drizzled over night, causing it to float away.

At school, no one reported seeing anything strange and the troublemakers certainly didn't want to bring up their failures, so they kept quiet about it.

Sammy and Wendy didn't want to say anything either, but hoped someday, they might see it again...

V. Outsmarting the Bullies

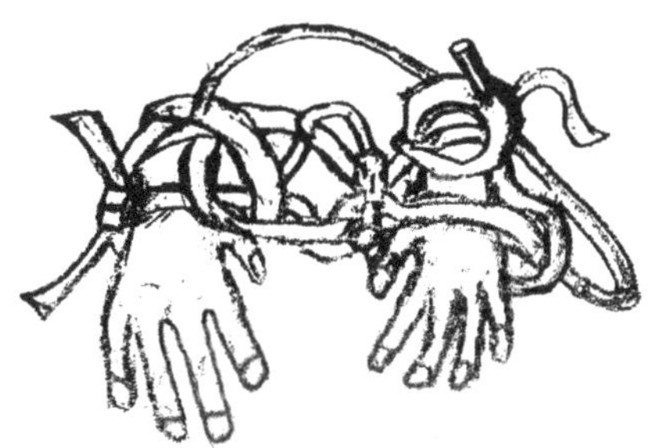

One week had gone by since the anti-gravity machine had been lost, but Sammy and Wendy were in good spirits. After school, they sat with their friends in the middle of the bus. Everyone was excited because it was finally the weekend. Even better, Brute and his pals weren't around because they were stuck in detention again.

"Hey, Jason, I heard that Max knocked over a trash can in the cafeteria and tried to blame it on the new kid," said Sammy.

"Yeah, looks like another unfortunate person for Brute and his gang to bother." Sammy turned towards Wendy and her friends. "Have any of you met the new kid?"

"Not yet, but I heard his name is Donovan, and he's nice looking... Uh, I mean a nice person," said Lisa, blushing.

Jason wasn't too thrilled to hear that because he kind of liked her. He called her a "giggle box" because she was always giggling. She had light, brown hair with a bob cut and was a little shorter than Wendy and Andrea. "I heard that he and his family moved into the old Shaker's house."

The bus stopped at the usual street corner and the kids stepped off one by one. Sammy and Wendy waved to their friends and walked home. It was only a few blocks ahead. They turned right onto a gravel road, which led them down a small hill in the direction of the town's lake.

Their house had a dirt driveway with an old wooden mailbox on the edge of the road. Various plants and weeds, including wild berries and sunflowers, grew around their house. There was also a large weeping willow in their front yard.

They raced to the door. "Hi, Mama! We're home!"

"Well, hello, darlings, how was school?"

"Oh, it was great. Brute and his friends were in detention again for bothering this new student, so we didn't have to deal with them on the bus," replied Sammy.

"I see. Well, wash up so you both can have some snacks," suggested Mrs. Flynn. She took care of the home while their father was at work.

Mr. Flynn was a supervisor at the tile factory. His team extracted granite from the stone quarries. He usually came home just before supper.

Wendy talked to her mother about the day's events. "I heard Donovan is nice, and his family moved into the old Shaker's house."

"Why don't you invite him over one day?"

"Sure, we'll ask him," she replied.

They both started their homework as their father pulled into to the driveway. He always checked the mailbox and picked up the newspaper just before coming inside.

"Hi, Pa, how was your day?" asked Wendy as she ran up to give him a hug.

"Hi, kiddos! It was okay. The guys at the quarry were a bit behind schedule because they decided to take a long lunch break." He changed his clothes and washed up for dinner.

Mrs. Flynn had cooked a spicy potato casserole with fresh asparagus on garlic fried rice. They all enjoyed the wonderful meal together.

The next morning, Sammy and Wendy decided to go to the park since it was a nice day with very few clouds in the sky.

"Wendy, go ahead of me, and I'll throw the Frisbee to you." With a whip of his hand, he flung the bright green disc to her. It curved in the air, but she was still able to catch it. Another kid approached the park as they were playing.

"Wendy, isn't that the new kid? Let's say hello." They both walked up to him. "Hi, you're Donovan, right?" Sammy asked.

"Yeah, I just moved here a few days ago," he replied with a strong accent.

"Nice. I'm Sammy, and this is my sister, Wendy. We live on Old Potters Lane. Where's your family from?"

"We're from Ireland. Our surname is O'Riley. My father was offered a job at the new steel factory as a craftsman. Our family has been in metallurgy for many generations."

"Hey, our family's heritage is Irish as well. Metallurgy? Does that mean an allergy to metals?" asked Wendy, confused.

"Oh, no, not at all. It's a science of purifying and producing higher quality metals. Sort of like alchemy. I really enjoy working with metal and wood," Donovan explained.

"That's neat. I like whittling sticks myself to create different shapes. I heard you had a run-in with Brute and his gang yesterday in school at lunch. What was that all about?" asked Sammy.

"Oh, yeah - that. Well, after I finished eating, I was about to throw away my trash when this kid pushed the trash can over and asked me to pick it up. Then, he knocked my tray to the ground and his taller friend kicked it. Finally, this large guy demanded my dessert. The cafeteria monitor saw the whole thing and sent them to the principal's office."

"Yeah, that was Brute, Max, and Zeek. Don't let those guys get to you. They've been trouble for years," said Sammy, recalling some bad memories from elementary school.

"Oh, I won't. I know just the solution for them. Would you both like to come to my house? I can show you my crafts."

"Okay, but we can only stay for a little while," Wendy said.

They followed Donovan to his house. He opened his fence door and they walked into his backyard.

They were amazed at what they saw. "Wow! You sure have a lot of tools and sculptures. Did you make all these yourself?" asked Sammy.

"Not everything. My father made the sculptures. I've been working on this special puzzle. Maybe you both would like to try it?" he asked, handing it to them.

"Yeah, sure!" Wendy replied. She really enjoyed puzzles.

Donovan made it from wood, string, and metal. It

had many twists and turns. He placed their hands in the holes and locked it. "Now, you have to try and get out of it," he challenged.

"Okay, it looks pretty easy, but I hope we don't break it," replied Sammy with concern.

"Oh, it won't break. You're welcome to try as hard as you want."

They struggled for five minutes, but were unable to break free from the special invention. "Uh, I don't think we can get out of this. Looks like you'll have to help us," Wendy requested.

"No problem." He simply tugged at a single metal link, and the entire contraption fell apart, freeing both of their hands in less than a second.

"That was amazing! How does it work?" asked Sammy.

"Well, you see, it's a family secret, but I'm glad you both enjoyed it. I plan to take it to school for presentation."

"Cool! Thanks for sharing it with us. Your family is very talented. We have to head home now, but we'll see you at the bus stop," said Wendy as they both waved goodbye.

Monday morning, they prepared their backpacks and lunches before heading to the bus stop.

Donovan was already there holding his invention. The other kids were curiously looking at it. They were about to ask him about it when Brute, Max, and Zeek showed up.

"Yo, check it out. That new kid we messed with last week is on our bus and he has some kind of artsy project with him," pointed out Max.

"Yeah, maybe we should make some improvements to it, if you know what I mean," snickered Zeek.

Brute just got out of detention, so he decided to be more careful in his approach. "Say, new kids, my pals and I was just foolin' arounds wich you at lunch there. No hard feelin's, right? Whatchya gots there?" he asked with a gleam in his eye.

Donovan was ready for them this time. "Oh, yeah, I'm fine. I'm Donovan, and this is my school project. You're welcome to look it over. Just be careful not to put your hands in the holes, or it might break," he cleverly replied, pretending to be worried.

Brute winked to his pals with a mischievous smile. All three of them quickly placed their hands in the holes and pulled back, hoping the contraption would break. Instead, it just locked them together.

"Ay'z! What happened heres? Takes it off, or I'll break your project in two," growled Brute.

Although the kids were excited that the bullies were locked up, they were careful not to laugh just in case they got loose.

"I'll wager that if you three can break out of it

before the bus comes, you can have it. Otherwise, you agree not to bother any of us for the rest of the week," negotiated Donovan.

Everyone anticipated Brute's response. He couldn't back down on any challenge in front of others.

"We'll breaks this alright, so I accepts your bet!"

Brute, Max, and Zeek made their best attempt to break free, but it was too strong. It hurt their hands each time they tried.

They could hear the bus coming around the corner as they continued to struggle. Time ran out and they had to give up. "Alright, Donny-boy, you win this round. Now, cuts us loose!" demanded Brute.

Donovan reached over and pulled at the small metal link, which immediately released their hands.

Although unhappy they failed the challenge, the boys were intrigued by his tricky contraption. Brute had a newfound respect for Donovan and kept his word by not bothering anyone for the rest of the week.

The word spread around school that Donovan had outsmarted the bullies with his talent. The kids realized that no matter how strange people may seem at first, everyone has something unique to contribute to the world. Donovan had no additional problems making friends or fitting in as the new kid.

VI. The Times Machine

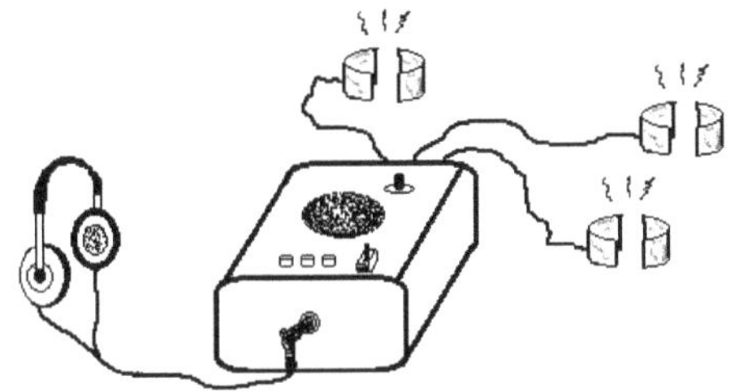

It was that time of the school year when the seventh and eighth graders at Old Greenwich Middle were required to participate in the science fair. This year's winner would receive a fully paid trip to NASA's space camp during spring break.

Sammy was nervous because he remembered how Wendy struggled the previous year on her project. Even so, he was excited to take on the challenge because he enjoyed being creative. He began to think of ideas in class while Mr. Beeker explained the rules.

"Hey, Jason, wanna be partners for the science fair?"

"Sure. Any ideas on what we can do?"

"Not yet, but come over after school and we can

figure it out."

Everyone turned their attention towards the back of the room after hearing a loud bang. Apparently, Zeek tried to catch a pencil that Brute tossed to him, but missed it, knocking his book to the floor instead.

"Mr. Kort, do we have a problem?" asked Mr. Beeker, raising his voice.

"Uh... No, sir. I just slipped trying to pick up my pencil," replied Zeek, embarrassed. Brute and Max mocked him.

As the teacher continued talking, Brute started to play a paper football game with Max and Zeek. He accidentally flicked it too hard, and it landed on another student's head. The student jumped out of his seat, thinking a bug had landed on his hair. The teacher looked over at the boys and knew exactly what was going on.

"Bruteus Baxter, are you done playing games?" asked Mr. Beeker in anger.

"Yeah, sure," he muttered.

"Let me remind you three that you will need to successfully complete a science fair project to get credit for this class, or you'll have to take it *again* next year!"

The three of them looked at each other with concern. Brute was aware that he would not be able to graduate middle school without passing science.

After class, Brute pulled his pals to the side of the hallway. "Yo, we needs a plan to gets this science project goin'. I don't wanna be stucks in this class again," he grumbled.

Max had a devious idea. "You know, Sammy's pretty smart. Let's get him to do it for us!"

"Yeah, good thinkin's, Max." The three of them followed Sammy to his locker.

"Yo, Sammy-boy, lemme haves a word wich you," requested Brute.

Sammy was surprised, but he was also curious about what they wanted.

"Yeah, we wanna talk to you," Zeek interjected, staring Sammy down.

Brute smacked him on his head. "Yo, Zeeko, lemme dooze the talkin's here! Now, as I was saying... You seez here, I gots me a problem and needs your help-"

"Hmm... So, what do you need?" asked Sammy.

"Old Beeker's got it out for us boys. If we'z don't pass the science fair, he's gonna holds me back. And I'm guessin' you wouldn't wants me around for a whole another year, right? So here's what's gonna happens... You'z gonna whip us up a real good projects, likes a times machine or sumpin' like that, or you'll be sharing your lunch with the three of us all next weeks!" He reached into Sammy's lunch bag and grabbed his Twinkie.

Although Sammy was reluctant to agree, he didn't feel like dealing with Brute's wrath and possibly being stuffed in his locker or losing his lunch and desserts for the entire week. "I understand your dilemma. I'll work on some ideas and get back to you."

"Yeah, that's what I means. We'll be seeing you soon..." replied Brute as the trio walked away.

Jason stood by and watched with anger. "Sammy, you're not going to let them get away with that, are you?"

"Not really. I have a few ideas for a '*times machine*' that might just knock their socks off!" Sammy winked.

"Ohhh... I get it. See you after school," smiled Jason as he headed to his next class.

Sammy started thinking about project ideas on the bus ride home. Wendy asked Andrea to be her partner for the science fair and invited her to come over as well.

Jason knew that Sammy liked Andrea and really enjoyed teasing him about it. She had wavy, light brown hair that floated around her shoulders and marble-like, blue eyes. She was a southern belle that transferred from a school called Peachtree Elementary in Georgia a few years back. Andrea was always nice and had a beautiful smile.

"Hey, Sammy, did you hear that? Looks like

Andrea is coming to your house too," he teased, stepping off the bus. Sammy pretended not to hear him and headed home.

Sammy and Wendy unloaded their bags, washed up, and started their homework.

"Andrea is coming over in an hour. We're going to work on our science fair project," said Wendy.

"Uh, okay," replied Sammy, starting to daydream. He forgot to tell her that Jason was also coming over.

After an hour, there was a knock at the door. Wendy went down to open it. "Oh, hi, Jason, come in. I thought you were Andrea. Sammy's upstairs."

"Cool," he replied, looking down, a bit shy.

Sammy came halfway down the stairs. "Hey, Jason, I heard your voice. Let's grab a snack first."

"Ohh... So you're just trying to stall time 'cause you wanna say hello to Andrea, right?"

"Uh, no. I... I usually like to have a quick snack after school," replied Sammy, unconvincingly. The two of them went into the kitchen.

After a few minutes, there was another knock at the door. Sammy's heart began to beat faster, knowing it must be Andrea. He was about to get up to open the door, but his knees wouldn't budge, so Wendy beat him to it.

"Hi, Andrea, come in. I'm so happy you're here! I have lots of ideas for our science fair project," chattered Wendy, giving her a quick hug.

Jason softly nudged Sammy out of the kitchen. "Oh, hey, Andrea. Uh, would you like a snack or something to rink? Uh, I mean drink?" stuttered Sammy as his tongue began to tangle.

"*Hiii,* Sammy. I'm good, but thank you!" she replied with a smile. She and Wendy headed upstairs, giggling.

"*Ohhh,* Sammmy... I would love to have a snack! And while you're at it, can you please wipe the crumbs off my face..." teased Jason in a girly voice as he began to laugh.

Sammy pushed him back into the kitchen. "Alright, Jason, enough with the jokes! Let's get our project started too," he replied, turning red in embarrassment.

"Oh, fine. Did you come up with something for Brute?"

"Yeah, but it's a surprise!"

"Okay, sounds like it's going to be a real winner, but what about our project?"

"Well, one idea would be to infuse helium into different types of super-conducting metals to see if we can get one to float. Or, we can create a holographic video game."

"Oh, definitely the game. It sounds like a lot of fun, and I think everybody will love it!"

"Great! Let's get to work then!"

Over the next few weeks, the boys worked hard on their project. Sammy also had to finish the bullies' project during the last few days before the science fair. He was exhausted, but he finally finished. He gathered up his supplies, and his father drove him to school so he could safely carry both projects.

Brute headed straight to Sammy's locker. Sammy was already there. "Yo, Sammy-boy! You'z weren't at the bus stops this mornin'. Thoughts ya might be duckin' us," he said, looking sternly at him.

"Oh, hey, Brute, I wouldn't do that. I built your time machine! I'll meet you at your locker before the science fair so I can show you how it works."

"Sounds good, and maybe we'll gets famous, eh?" asked Brute, feeling proud in the moment.

"Oh, sure. You three will get real popular... Well, at least in our school. I have to get to class now, but I'll see you later."

Walking to class, Sammy smiled, imagining how popular the three of them would be when the judges viewed their presentation.

Wendy and Andrea also finished their project. They decided to see which type of music would help their plants grow healthier.

Just before the science fair, Sammy approached Jason's locker. "Hey, Jason, here's our project. Go ahead and set everything up. I have to meet up with

Brute and his gang. Wish me luck!"

"Yeah, you're gonna need it. And don't worry, I have everything under control for our awesome project!" replied Jason. He was curious to see what Sammy created for the bullies, but would have to wait for their presentation.

Sammy headed over to Brute's locker. The trio was anxiously waiting for him. "Yo, Sammy, thoughts ya might not shows up. Luckies you gots here in time," said Brute, eyes narrowing.

"Of course, guys. I always keep my word. Here it is." He handed him a box the size of a briefcase with buttons and straps on it. "You need to pay close attention now. When the judges tell you to go on stage, place these electric straps on your wrists and hold each other's hands. Then put these headphones on. Once you're ready, press this button, and the headphones will guide you after that. It should take you into the future by a few minutes," explained Sammy with sweet sincerity.

"Uh, okay, sounds real easy. Max... Zeek... Grabs it! And let's gets the shows on the road!" demanded Brute. He actually felt pretty good about himself.

Max was skeptical, but he didn't want to rock the boat.

"Hey, Max, do you think I'll rule the school in the future?" asked Zeek.

Brute slapped his head as the three of them walked to the cafeteria. "Ain't no ones ruling this school buts me!" he declared.

Other students were busy setting up their projects as they entered the cafeteria. Most of them were surprised to see the trio and curious about what they planned to present.

Mr. Beeker walked up on stage and announced that Wendy and Andrea would be first to present.

Wendy introduced their project and Andrea showed how the plants that they exposed to classical music looked healthier than the ones they exposed to hard rock.

Sammy paid extra close attention when Andrea spoke. Everyone applauded as they left the stage. Mr. Beeker called Sammy and Jason to present next.

They stepped onto the stage and Sammy explained to the judges that they had built a holographic video game. Everyone watched with interest as the boys sat in chairs across from each other.

Brute and his pals also watched intently, thinking that Sammy's project could not be as revolutionary as theirs.

Jason flipped a switch on his controller, and all of a sudden, images of enemy space ships appeared in mid-air between the two of them. The crowd was amazed. The two of them began to fire missiles at each other's ships. Points were also displayed in mid-air. Jason ultimately won the battle.

No one had ever seen a holographic video game before. Their demonstration was a hit! Everyone clapped. They stepped down from the stage while the judges thanked them for their exciting presentation.

"Yo, Brute, that game sure was cool. I hope the judges like our project too," commented Max, feeling a bit nervous.

Brute was still confident that their project would be even more amazing.

Mr. Beeker called the three of them onto the stage. He was impressed that they actually completed a project and showed up to present it.

They walked onto the stage with big smiles. Brute turned towards the crowd and announced, "Ay, you'z all out there, we'z got a real treats here for ya! My boys and I are abouts to travel into the future with our times machine!"

The judges and Mr. Beeker heard him say "*times machine*" and assumed they created a new type of multiplication calculator.

The troublemakers placed the electric straps on their wrists and put on their headphones. Everyone laughed, seeing the three bullies holding hands with each other. But of course, they couldn't hear the crowd with their headphones on.

"Alright, Max! Hits that buttons now!" instructed Brute, speaking louder than normal.

Max hit it, and they started to hear trance-like music with a monotonous countdown coming through their headphones. They began to get sleepy and entered into a hypnotic state.

At the end of the first minute, the time machine issued a command that told Brute to kick Zeek, Zeek to kick Max, and Max to kick Brute. They kicked each other so hard that it knocked their socks off. They continued kicking every three seconds for a full minute as the crowd laughed hysterically.

In the last minute, the machine made them forget everything that happened. When they finally awoke, the crowd was cheering with tears of laughter.

The boys believed they had successfully traveled into the future by a few minutes and everyone loved their presentation. The trio bowed as they limped off the stage not knowing why their legs were hurting so much.

Mr. Beeker stepped up and reached for the microphone. "Well, that was the most unusual science fair project I've ever seen. I have to say, it was not only entertaining, but it may be useful for disciplining kids some day in the future. We thank you for your presentation, and you'll be happy to know that you will receive full credit! You boys may want to head to the nurses office," kindly instructed

Mr. Beeker, proud of their accomplishment.

The judges were ready to announce the winners of this year's science fair. Third place went to Abigail and Deborah for developing a new lipstick that would last an entire week, even if washed.

To everyone's surprise, Brute, Max, and Zeek were awarded second place for developing a solution that could be used by teachers to discipline naughty kids.

Finally, first place went to Sammy and Jason for their advanced holographic gaming system. They were awarded entry to NASA's space camp.

Brute and his pals were ecstatic about passing science class and even winning an award. Since they never found out what really happened to them, they didn't bother Sammy for the rest of the month.

Even though Sammy was hoping to teach them a lesson, he realized that doing good deeds for others could also lead to a positive result.

Sammy and Jason were really happy that they would be going to space camp during spring break. All of their friends and teachers congratulated them on their achievement.

VII. Space Camp

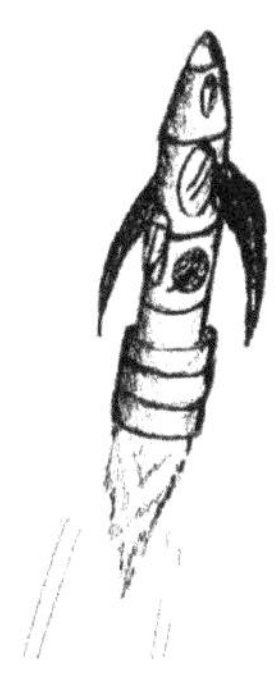

Sammy spent the last few days just before spring break finishing his school assignments. He and Wendy were really excited about being totally free from homework, even if it was for a little while. Wendy was looking forward to just hanging out with her friends.

This break was going to be extra special because Sammy and Jason had won first place in the science fair for creating a holographic video game. The school was sending them to NASA's two-week space camp. He only had one day to prepare for the trip.

"Hi, Mama, we're home!"

"Well, hello, my darlings! How was your day?"

"It was great! We're free! Yippee!" shouted Wendy.

"Wonderful. Sammy, you and Jason are off to space camp this weekend. Isn't it exciting?" asked Mrs. Flynn.

"Yeah, I have to pack some books, games, and survival gear just in case we have to make a trip into space," he grinned.

"Well, I hope you plan on packing your clothes, socks, and underwear too because it might get chilly in space," teased Wendy.

"Haha, I think I'm fine with that."

The next night, Sammy prepared for his trip. He and Jason got together to plan their activities at camp. As part of their prize, the school gave them a t-shirt with *NASA* written in big bold letters, and *Space Camp* written just below it. There was also a picture of a large rocket on it.

The family sat down for their last dinner together before the trip. "You're very lucky to be going to space camp. Very few kids get this opportunity," commended his father.

Wendy eagerly listened. "Does this mean I can have his room *all* to myself, and invite my friends for a sleep over?"

"Pa, please make sure Wendy and her friends

don't mess up my room while I'm gone," pleaded Sammy.

"Oh, don't worry, we'll look after it. You just make sure you enjoy camp. We're going to miss you," added Mrs. Flynn.

"I'll miss you too, but it's only two weeks. I'll be back safe and sound before you know it."

That night, Sammy was anxious and couldn't get to sleep right away, so he started to imagine flying through space to another galaxy. Eventually, he got drowsy and fell into a deep slumber.

He started dreaming about an electromagnetic propulsion pack that he built from a microwave to fly to the moon. It was odd, but he could see his mother standing on the moon calling out to him.

It was early morning and Mrs. Flynn had just entered his room. She whispered, "Sammy, Sammy... It's time to get up. You need to quickly get ready, so we can make it to the bus station on time."

All of a sudden, he realized he wasn't dreaming. He woke up, but couldn't remember what he was dreaming about. For some reason, he started thinking about warming up a breakfast patty in the microwave. He stretched his arms and headed to the bathroom.

Wendy kept sleeping until she heard the toilet flush. She remembered Sammy would be leaving for camp, so she forced herself up and headed down for breakfast.

Mrs. Flynn had prepared Sammy's favorite dishes: hash browns, waffles, toast, and links. She was packing his lunch when she heard a knock at the door.

"Come in, Jason. Would you like to have breakfast with us?" she kindly asked.

"Good morning, Mrs. Flynn. Thank you, I'd love to. Hey, Sammy! Hi, Wendy!"

After eating a wonderful breakfast, they loaded the car. Wendy gave Sammy a hug and was sad to see him leave, but also excited for him.

"Safe journey, boys, we'll miss you!" said Mrs. Flynn, waving goodbye.

"Buckle up, boys, we're ready to lift off!" chuckled Mr. Flynn with a big smile.

They arrived at the station and could see a huge bus with a *NASA Space Camp* logo on it. There were many other kids already standing in line to board.

"Alright, boys, don't forget your stuff and have a great trip! I'll pick you up here in two weeks," stated Mr. Flynn.

"Alright, Pa, love you!"

"Bye, Mr. Flynn, and thanks for the ride!" shouted Jason, dragging his bags to where the group of kids and a young lady in charge were standing.

She was a NASA space camp leader who recently

graduated from college with a degree in physics and astronomy. She seemed friendly.

"Hello, kids! My name is Julie Sern, and I'll be your guide. Please put your bags in the baggage compartment and line up to board the rocket bus!"

Sammy and Jason were relieved to have made it just in time. They got in line and noticed all the kids seemed to be very polite. There were no bullies around for once.

A short, cute girl with dark hair and round glasses walked up behind them. She was quite pepped up.

"Hey, guys! I'm Emma! I won first place in my school's science fair by proving that the speed of light was needed as the fourth dimension in Einstein's field equations for general relativity!"

"That sounds really complex. Glad to meet you, Emma. I'm Sammy, and this is my best friend, Jason. We created a holographic video game."

"That's wild! I *luuvvv* video games! I just have to try it someday," she replied.

Jason was intrigued, but a little shy to figure out what to say next, so he just smiled.

"Okay, everyone, please be careful as you step onto the bus," instructed Ms. Sern. All the kids boarded.

It was no ordinary bus. Each of the seats had a control panel and screen. The roof looked like a planetarium with images of constellations and planets. Even the driver's section looked like a cockpit.

Once everyone was seated, the bus driver stood up and announced, "Welcome aboard, rocket fans! As we prepare to lift off, make sure your seat belts are securely buckled and your control panels are switched on!"

With the flip of a switch, the bus driver closed all the window shades, and each of the seats began to vibrate. The kids watched their screen and heard a countdown from the loudspeaker. When it reached zero, the driver yelled, "Blastoff!" They all felt like they were lifting off as the bus began to move.

During the first hour of the ride, Ms. Sern talked about the constellation of Orion projected on the roof and the possibility of undiscovered planets in other solar systems.

"Okay, kids, we're in the last thirty minutes of our ride, so go ahead and hit the launch button on your control panel," she said. With their seats tilted back, they hit the button. Suddenly their screens turned on and joysticks popped out from their armrests. It was a video game of a rocket flying towards the moon! The challenge was to safely land the rocket. That was the most exciting bus ride they ever had.

The bus driver opened the shades when they reached their final destination. After being in the dark for so long, the kids had to cover their eyes to adjust to the sunlight again. There was a large NASA space camp sign and a huge rocket in the middle of the courtyard.

Ms. Sern told everyone to step off the rocket bus and grab their bags. She led them all through the main building's entrance.

"Alright, kids! I hope you enjoyed the ride, but now it's time to go to your assigned quarters, so please review the register to find your room. Take a few minutes to relax and unpack, and I'll meet you all in the cafeteria in an hour."

Sammy and Jason were in deep concentration looking for their assigned room on the wall when Emma approached them from behind.

"Wow! That bus was awesome, wasn't it?"

The boys quickly turned around. "Oh, hi, Emma, yeah, we really enjoyed it. We're in the blue hall. How about you?" asked Jason, hoping she might be in the same hall.

"My room is in the red hall. See y'all later," cheerily said Emma, skipping away.

Sammy and Jason found their room halfway down the hallway. Sammy placed his hand on the wall panel, triggering the door to open. It was exactly like he had seen on *Star Trek*.

"Jason, this is really cool. It's like being on the *Enterprise*. I can't wait to see what's next."

"Yeah, this is awesome! Even the space books on this shelf are really cool."

After relaxing a bit, the boys headed to the cafeteria. Most of the other kids were already there. It looked like a replica of the *Enterprise's* "Ten Forward" café'.

"Hey, guys! What did you think about your rooms and this far out cafeteria?" asked Emma, suddenly popping out from behind them.

"Uh, Emma, why do you keep sneaking up on us like that?" asked Sammy, surprised to see her again.

"Oh, I'm just stealthy like that. What do you two have in your lunch bags? I'm hungry!" Emma was a quick talker and generally curious about many things.

Jason was happy to respond. "Oh, my mom packed me the usual sandwich, chips, fruit, dessert, and a drink. Would you like to sit with-" he started to offer.

Emma had already sat down before he could finish asking. He was taking a liking to her. Sammy thought she was nice, but a little hyperactive.

"Hello, everyone, again! We are very glad to have you all here this spring. You will be happy to know that there will be a real space shuttle launch tomorrow! After lunch, I'll take everyone to the launch bay," announced Ms. Sern.

Sammy, Jason, and Emma lined up for the tour. They were part of the first group of kids to take the elevator up to the platform level to reach the shuttle's entrance. The entire craft was attached vertically to two very tall rocket boosters at least twenty stories high.

Jason looked down from the railing. "Oh, man! We're really high up!" he said, cringing. He wasn't too fond of heights.

Emma entered the side door first. The boys followed her. She was anxious to see what was inside. "I spent a lot of time studying shuttle design and something doesn't seem right... Ah-ha! The main cockpit is missing!" chimed Emma.

Ms. Sern overheard her comment. "You're very perceptive, Emma. Good for you! The cockpit had a malfunction, and the engineers are working on it now. It should be ready for the launch tomorrow morning."

That evening, Sammy and Jason were busy reading some books when the door entry bell dinged.

"Enter!" exclaimed Sammy, feeling like Captain Picard of the *Enterprise*. The door slid open. It was Emma.

"Hey, guys! Watchya doing? I'm really bored. Wanna go exploring?"

"Uh, are we allowed to roam around on our own?" asked Jason.

"Well, no one said we couldn't. I'll be your guide. Follow me!" She grabbed their hands and pulled them up.

"I guess we have to follow our guide," said Jason with a smile. They walked out with her.

"Where are we headed?" asked Sammy, worried they might get into trouble.

"Don't worry, you'll see..." They turned right at the corner, and could see a large double door with a sign that displayed *Shuttle Simulation Room*.

Opening the doors, they entered a large engineering laboratory. There was a shuttle simulator in the middle of the room. It was a huge box-like structure propped up by four large hydraulic cylinders. Jason looked around the room. "Uh, I'm not sure we should be in here, but it's really interesting," he whispered.

"Well, we're here, so let's make the best of it! Look at those space suits on the wall. Oh, it's so tempting... We just have to put them on. Come on, guys, let's be like real astronauts!" insisted Emma.

Sammy had a feeling they might get into trouble, but he couldn't pass up a once-in-a-lifetime opportunity to try on a real space suit at NASA. Besides, what harm could there be in wearing it for a few minutes?

They put the suits on and jumped into the simulator. Emma was proud to have read books about space shuttles. She already knew how to start one.

The three of them were unaware that the real cockpit was being repaired in the lab next door. The engineers were working on it while the astronauts trained in preparation for the early morning launch.

Emma fired up the simulator, but had no idea it was linked to the real cockpit. They spent time enjoying the simulation training exercises.

Suddenly, a glitch in the real cockpit caused their door to lock. The three of them were stuck inside, and all of the systems shut down.

The engineers started troubleshooting the problem. One of them addressed the flight crew leader. "Sir, it appears that one of your control boards has malfunctioned. We'll try to fix it from here, but if we can't, we may have to postpone the launch."

The senior astronaut heard him, but could not reply because his out-bound communication panel was disabled.

Meanwhile in the simulator, Emma was also trying to call out for help, but her communication signal was jammed.

"How do we get out of here?" asked Sammy, convinced their late night rendezvous was a bad idea.

"It looks like all systems are down according to the last incoming message. We'll have to wait for a re-boot," she replied.

After some time had passed, they were tired of waiting and fell asleep.

The engineers continued working all night and eventually fixed everything. The astronauts were finally able to leave and get some rest. The lead engineer was exhausted from all the late-night work, so he gave his team instructions to load the cockpit into the shuttle before heading off to sleep.

One of the junior engineers on his team was new to the program and didn't have much experience. The other team members decided to leave him in charge anyway because they were hungry and left for breakfast.

With no one around to guide him, the junior engineer accidentally entered the wrong cockpit pickup request, which caused the crane to clamp down on the simulator instead of the real cockpit.

It began to shake as it disengaged from the hydraulic legs. Sammy, Jason, and Emma suddenly woke up as the crane began to lift them up.

"Uh, what was that?" asked Jason, surprised.

"Maybe the system is coming back online and we can finally get out of here!" shouted Sammy.

Emma stared out the window. "Hmm... Not so fast! We seem to be rising, and there are no lights on the panel yet," she noted with suspicion.

A few minutes later, they felt a thud as the crane released the simulator onto the shuttle bay. Once it was locked in place, the panel lights began to turn on one by one.

"Hey, I think this is it. We should be able to get out now, right, Emma?" nervously asked Jason. Just then, the auto-sequencing instructions warned them to pressurize their suits and fasten their seat belts. "Or, maybe not?"

"Let's follow the instructions. Maybe I can perform a manual release to get us out," she suggested.

The three of them buckled in and set their suits to high-pressure mode. They began to hear the computer count down. Emma attempted to stop it, hoping to open their door, but the computer responded that it was incapable of accepting manual commands or communication requests during a shuttle launch.

"I'm beginning to get a *b-baaad* feeling about this," she stuttered.

"Emma... What's going on?" asked Sammy.

"Uh, I'm not sure, but I-" She tried to respond, but the entire simulator began to shake even more. The rocket boosters ignited and the tower clamps released, allowing the shuttle to start lifting off.

All of the other kids from camp were watching the launch from the control tower. They could see the massive flames spreading beneath the rocket boosters.

Inside the shuttle, the three kids began to feel the g-force increase tremendously as it accelerated upward. "Emma, Emma... Are we lifting off?"

sputtered Jason as his cheeks began to flutter.

"Oh gosh! Here we go!" she yelled.

"What do you mean, '*Here we go?*' And where exactly are we going?" asked Sammy, panicking.

"Don't look now, but I think we're heading to outer space! That's not the simulator screen, it's a real window!" Emma screamed.

Within a few minutes, they escaped Earth's gravitational boundary and entered space. The on-board computer was controlling their trajectory. Their panel showed the rocket boosters disengaging and falling back to the earth.

"Wow! This is the coolest experience of my life!" said Emma in awe.

"Yeah, and look at how amazing the Earth looks!" exclaimed Sammy, staring out the window.

"I see it! It's so blue and perfect," added Jason.

For a moment, the control tower's crew thought the launch was a success. They were about to turn on communications to request status, when the real astronauts walked in.

"Hey, guys! Sorry we're late. We got stuck in training last night and had to grab some breakfast this morning, so we apologize for delaying the launch," expressed the senior astronaut.

"Uh, launch delay? What launch delay? We already launched! And if you're here, and not in there, then who's in the space shuttle??" asked the lead engineer with a horrified look as he turned towards his team for answers.

"Sir, I can explain. I'm really sorry, but I'm new and I think I accidentally entered the wrong pickup request code. Apparently, the simulator is on the shuttle. I, I... don't *think* anyone is on board," stammered the junior engineer.

"How's that possible? Where was the rest of your team?" the lead engineer demanded.

"Well, they were really hungry and-" the junior engineer attempted to respond, but was cut off by the sound of an incoming communication.

"Hello... Hello... Can anyone hear us?" cried Sammy.

"Oh my goodness! There are kids on board! I think they're part of the space camp group. Get Ms. Sern in here. Stat!" ordered the lead engineer.

While waiting for her to come, he spoke to the children. "Kids, if you can hear me, please tell me your names and how you got on board."

"Roger that! I'm Emma, the captain of this shuttle, and I have my co-pilots, Sammy Flynn, and Jason Smith, on board too. We wanted to try out the simulator last night and got locked in when the systems went down. We fell asleep waiting for your engineers to fix it. The next thing we knew, we were lifting off. Now we're watching Earth from outer space! Woo-hoo!!" she rattled off in one breath.

"Okay, okay... Don't be scared. We're trying to come up with a plan to bring you all safely back. Everything will be fine," replied the lead engineer with a drop of sweat rolling down his cheek.

"Scared? Who's scared? In fact, I have over eight hundred hours of training on this shuttle!" boasted Emma.

"Eight hundred hours? Which department trained you?"

"Well, you see... It was Macrozap's virtual reality department!" She replied in a professional tone.

The lead engineer turned to his team. "Does anyone know who runs that department?"

The junior engineer raised his hand. "Yeah, that's an awesome video game. The last time I played, I scored-" he started to say, remembering his gaming days.

The lead engineer cut him off and spoke into the microphone. "So, you're telling me that your training has only been on a video game??" he asked with a few more drops of sweat on his forehead.

"Uh, yes, sir!" she cheerily responded.

He muted the panel and turned to his team. "I think we're in big trouble here. We had better keep this situation under wraps until we have a solution!"

Back on the shuttle, Emma turned to the boys.

"Now that we're on auto-pilot and in proper orbit, let's unbuckle," instructed Emma as she removed her belt and began to float around.

"Hey, that looks like fun. I'd like to give it a whirl," said Jason as he tried unbuckling too. "Sammy, I can't get this off! Can you help?"

"Sure. Luckily, I brought my trusty pocketknife," he said, releasing his belt.

"Here I come!" he shouted, floating towards Jason. Sammy used his knife to unlatch Jason's belt.

Feeling weightless, Jason began to wonder. "Why do we float in space anyway?" he asked, slowly turning upside down in the air.

"We're not actually floating. We're constantly falling at the same speed that the shuttle is falling around Earth's gravitational field, so it just seems like we're floating," explained Emma, pretending to be Super Girl.

They were having the time of their lives when suddenly an alarm sounded with a red, blinking light.

Emma floated back to the panel and pressed the communication button. "Houston, I think we have a problem! Oh gosh, I always wanted to say that," she chuckled.

"We hear you. We have an indication that your guidance system has malfunctioned. We're working on the solution now!" gasped the lead engineer.

Ms. Sern entered the room. "For heaven's sake, are those my students in space you're talking to?"

"Yes, Ma'am, we're very sorry. It's a long story, but you'd better have a seat because we're in the middle of another crisis!" he replied after a new incoming alarm sounded.

Emma interrupted. "Uh, engineer, boss man? I don't mean to make things more complicated, but I think we have a bigger problem. My radar screen indicates the shuttle is on a collision course with the INMAR satellite. I'm going to have to switch to manual to get us back on track!"

The team huddled for a quick discussion. "Emma, you're right. It's the best chance you have. It's up to you all now to save yourselves. Our thoughts are with you," said the lead engineer.

"Guys, we'd better buckle up! The ride is about to get rough!" she instructed.

They quickly floated back down towards their seats and fastened their belts.

"Sammy, you'll need to control the speed on my mark! Jason, you'll need to read the trajectory coordinates and elevation status back to me every ten seconds while I steer us to safety!" Emma switched to manual mode and grabbed the flight stick.

"Jason! Drop elevation by five hundred feet. Sammy! Reduce our speed by ten percent by engaging the reverse thrusters for three seconds!"

"Aye aye, captain! Elevation down and gradient locked!" replied Jason.

"Reverse thrusters engaged and holding for three seconds!" shouted Sammy.

Emma began to bank the shuttle left towards Earth to avoid the satellite. The engineering team, flight crew, and Ms. Sern listened intently. They were shocked that she knew exactly what to do to get the shuttle back on course.

"Guys, get ready!" she shouted. "We're crossing Earth's boundary in 'T' minus five seconds. Sammy! Engage the thrusters at maximum and hold for five seconds! We're going to spiral around the earth and gradually drop in elevation to minimize friction burn. Gravity will take care of the rest for us. We're going in for a landing, so hang on to your lunch!"

Their cheeks began to ripple as gravity accelerated the shuttle. It was like being on a fast, free-fall ride at the amusement park.

The guidance system came back on as soon as they entered the atmosphere. Emma switched to autopilot, and the space shuttle landed safely on NASA's runway tarmac.

Apparently, the communication between the control tower and the space shuttle had been intercepted by news reporters. They broadcast the story to live television and radio across the world.

Sammy, Jason, and Emma became immediate

celebrities for being the youngest astronauts to fly into space and safely land a space shuttle. They were awarded medals of honor and even had their pictures framed on NASA's wall of fame.

Space camp was way beyond what Sammy had ever imagined, but he would cherish those memories for a long time. He and Jason promised to stay in touch with Emma.

The boys realized that not following the rules landed them in a lot of hot water, but they were relieved to have made it safely back home. The two of them became the most popular kids in school for at least the first few weeks after the break.

VIII. Magic Beans

Mrs. Flynn usually made hash browns every Sunday morning, but Sammy couldn't smell any cooking when he woke up. He was craving it, so he went downstairs to see if his mother was planning to make some.

"Morning, Mama."

"Good morning. Is Wendy still sleeping?"

"I think so. She had her head covered when I left the room. I'm starving. Can you please make some hash browns for breakfast?"

"Sorry, Sammy, we ran out of it last weekend, and I didn't get a chance to go to the grocery store."

"Oh. Can I go and buy some?"

"Sure, if you really want." Mrs. Flynn handed him some money.

"Absolutely! I'll be back in a jiffy! Love you! Bye!" he shouted, running out the door.

Sammy trotted over to the corner market. It was not too far from his house. He was about to enter when he noticed an old man with a cane stumbling towards a bench just outside the store. He seemed quite out of breath. Sammy didn't want him to fall, so he quickly ran up to him. "Can I help you to the bench, sir?"

"Oh, sure, sonny, thank you very much. I haven't eaten in days, and I'm losing my strength," quivered the old man as he struggled to sit.

Sammy felt sad and wanted to buy him some food, but he only had enough money for hash browns. After thinking some more, he felt compelled to help the old man. "Sir, why don't you rest here, and I'll bring you some food and water," he said politely.

Sammy quickly entered the market store and bought a small sandwich and bottle of water. He was hungry too, but it didn't matter to him anymore. He walked back out and handed the items to the old man.

"Oh, you're a real angel, young sonny. I really appreciate this." The old man gobbled up the sandwich and chugged the water. "Since you have been so nice to me, I'm going to give you some of my magic beans."

He reached into his back pocket and pulled several of them out. "Now listen here. These beans have powerful magic that can help you when you need it, but don't eat more than one a day. Heed my warning, and eat only one bean a day!" echoed the old man. He placed seven small beans onto Sammy's hand.

"Thank you, sir! I understand and will remember what you said." Sammy ran home, excited.

His mother was anxiously awaiting his return. "What took you so long?" she asked with concern.

"Well, Mama, I had to help this old man. He was hungry and weak. I had to use the money you gave me to buy him a sandwich and water. And in return, he gave me these magic beans!" Sammy panted as he opened his hand to show her.

"It's really nice of you to help the elderly, but I'm also concerned that he might have tricked you into buying him food. These beans look pretty ordinary."

"Well, I'd like to keep them anyway." He placed them in his school bag.

Wendy was busy finishing her breakfast and overheard their conversation. "Hmmm... Magic beans, eh? Sounds like a story I've heard before..." She giggled.

Sammy ignored her comment and finished his breakfast.

After doing chores, he and Wendy played board games for the rest of the day.

The next morning, Sammy packed his books, lunch, and P.E. clothes. He wasn't looking forward to gym class today because his team was scheduled to play basketball against Brute's team. He was getting nervous just thinking about it, but at least he would have his friends Jason and Brandon on his side.

At the bus stop, Jason walked up to him. "Hey, Sammy, you know what day it is?"

"Yeah, I know. We'll just have to do our best to score at least once," he replied with a frown.

Brute overheard what Sammy had said and walked up behind him. "You'z squeakers can keeps on dreamin'. When I see you'z two on the courts today, I'm gonna picks you ups and dunks you in the net!"

Luckily, the heavy sound of the bus that was pulling around the corner distracted him. Boarding first was more important for Brute.

Max and Zeek were running late, but still managed to catch the door before it closed. They taunted Sammy and Jason about the basketball game the entire way to school.

The first part of his day went well, but it was finally time for P.E. The gym was on the other side of the school. As Sammy walked through the hallway, he began to imagine how nice it would be to have a rocket scooter to whip down the halls.

Sammy met Jason in the boys locker room. He remembered that he had the magic beans in his bag. He reached in and pulled one out. "Hey, Jason, ready for the game?"

"I guess so."

"I wish I had the skills of a pro basketball player." Sammy popped the bean in his mouth. He hoped it would give him just a little extra energy.

"Yeah, we're going to need all the help we can get!"

During warm up, Sammy felt a sudden surge of energy. He began to dribble faster, passing the ball from one hand to the other as he ran towards the basket. He felt like he had hawk eyes as he jumped and tossed the ball into the basket with super precision. Somehow he knew it would go in.

Jason and the rest of his team were shocked.

"Say, Sammy, where did you learn those moves?" asked Brandon.

"It must be the Koco Krunchers I ate this morning. I feel great!" He knew it was really the magic bean, but he didn't want to say that. His attention began to sway towards the bleachers.

The girls were waiting for their turn to play. Sammy could see Andrea watching his team practice from a distance. He didn't want to be obvious by staring at her, so he quickly glanced away. He couldn't mess up this game in front of her.

The gym teacher, Coach Harrison, asked the two teams to start playing.

Brute was wearing a dark, burgundy bandana with a cutoff t-shirt. He sure looked menacing. He might have been strong but he was a bit slower than the rest of his team. Zeek was tall, but didn't always pay attention when playing basketball.

Both teams entered the court. Brute stared down at Sammy's team. "Y'all are going *dowwwnn...*" he growled.

Sammy's team nudged him to the center position for the jump off. He was a bit reluctant, but had to maintain his composure. All he could think about was Andrea watching him from the bleachers. Unfortunately, he had to jump against Zeek, who towered over him.

Coach Harrison held the ball up high in one hand. There was a moment of silence just before he blew his whistle and tossed up the orange ball.

With all his might, Sammy jumped, stretching his hand as far up as he could. To his surprise, he actually reached the ball first. He quickly knocked it towards Jason who was too nervous to hold on to it, so he tossed the ball back to Sammy as fast as he could.

Sammy was barely ready for it, but with his heightened senses, he grabbed the ball and made his way right past the defense.

He dribbled forward, backward, under his legs, and around his waist. He could feel the extra power in his jump, which lifted him through the air as he spun and threw the ball towards the basket. It arced, and with a swish, it dropped straight into the net.

After momentary shock and silence from the crowd, Sammy could hear everyone begin to clap and cheer.

Both teams were surprised at his moves, including the gym teacher. "Hey, Sammy, that was awesome! I never knew you could play ball like that!" His team members gave him a high five.

Brute's team was still in denial. He knocked Zeek upside his head. "Pay attentions! How could you'z let that pint-size, pro wannabe gets the ball likes that?"

Puzzled, he said, "Sorry, Brute, I don't know what happened. We'll get 'em on the next point!" Zeek took the ball back to the starting line and threw it to his team member who immediately tossed it to Brute.

He started to dribble with one of his big hands out in front of him to block other players. Sammy's team just watched in fear as he made his way down the court.

Sammy yelled out to his team to block, but no one had the nerve to try. Brute took a free shot and watched in glory as it dropped into the net. He scored two points for his team. "Now, that's how you'z do it!" he shouted, beaming the ball to Brandon.

Brandon took the basketball behind the line and passed it to Sammy. Brute attempted to block, but before he could reach him, Sammy turned around in a snap and dribbled past him with a layup to the net. He spun the ball up with ease, and it bounced off the backboard, falling directly into the net.

"Score!" yelled the coach. Sammy's team was ahead by two points.

Brute's team continued to play a tough game. As much as they tried to stop Sammy, they couldn't catch him. Brute and Zeek really worked up a sweat.

The game ended ten to two. Sammy's team had won by a landslide! Everyone cheered from the bleachers. It made him feel like he was on top of the world.

Brute was furious and threw the basketball at the wall. To his dismay, it bounced off and hit Coach Harrison's behind. Zeek started to laugh, but the rest of the crowd stared in shock.

The gym teacher was very angry and told them to stay after school for detention and clean all of the sweaty gym equipment.

Sammy walked back to the locker room with Jason

and told him about the magic beans. Neither of them were aware that Max was eavesdropping from the other side of their locker.

Max couldn't believe what he heard, but if there was any truth to what Sammy said, then he would have to find a way to get the beans. He began devising a plan.

The news of Sammy's team winning the game quickly spread throughout school.

At the end of the day, Andrea walked up to Sammy's locker with a smile. "*Hiii,* Sammy! You really played a great game today!"

Being shy in the moment, his memory began to lock. "Game? Oh, right, the game. Yeah, I just got lucky, I guess."

"Lucky? You were really great out there." She walked with him to the bus.

Andrea ran up to his sister. "Hi, Wendy! Did you hear about Sammy's team winning basketball today?"

"I sure did. I also heard that Brute and Zeek are in detention for being sore losers," happily replied Wendy. "Awesome job, bro. Uh, hello..., Sammy?"

He was still on cloud nine from walking with Andrea all the way to the bus. All he could think about was her compliment. "Uh, sorry, what did you say?"

"I said awesome job for beating Brute's team!"

During dinner that evening, Sammy started telling his parents about the game when he suddenly felt tired. He fell asleep earlier than normal.

With great difficulty, he woke up the next morning, completely drained. Apparently, the magic bean took a lot of energy out of him the previous day. He began to think it wasn't such a good thing after all, especially after remembering the condition of the old man that gave him the beans. He dragged himself out of bed and made it down for breakfast even though his head was hurting.

After getting ready for school, Sammy struggled to keep up with Wendy on their way to the bus stop. They could see Brute, Max, and Zeek coming around the corner.

Max was busy telling his pals about what he had learned. "We need to get a hold of those beans," he said urgently. Although Brute found it hard to believe, it was a good reason to create trouble, so he agreed to help.

Max walked up to Sammy. "Yo, Sammy, looks like Brute left his lunch money at home, and he doesn't wanna go hungry today, so let's see what you got in that backpack of yours!" he demanded.

"Okay, but I don't have much." Sammy pulled out his bag of beans, thinking they wouldn't be interested. "This is all I have. I don't think he's going to like it much."

"Get a load of this! He's got a bag of healthy beans," said Zeek, sarcastically winking.

"Funny, I was just cravings sumpin' healthy," said Brute.

Max took all six beans out of the bag. He kept two and divided the rest between Brute and Zeek.

"Now, guys... Don't eat-" Sammy tried to warn.

All three of them immediately gobbled them up before he could tell them about eating only one per day.

"Them beans sure tasted good. Now, we'll seez who's gonna win the rest of the games this week!" boasted Brute.

The bus pulled up and the three boarded first as usual. Suddenly, they could feel a lot of energy building up inside them as they sat in the back. They were beginning to feel some heavy rumblings in their stomachs.

As soon as they reached the school, the troublemakers rushed down the hall to find the nearest boy's bathroom. Everyone could hear some pretty harsh sounds coming from in there.

For the rest of the day, wherever the trio went, they expressed a lot of gassy troubles. The kids could not believe their ears or their noses. Even the teacher noticed and sent the three to the nurse's office.

Brute was mad again. But this time, he was angry

with Max. "Why'd ya makes us eat them beans this mornin'? We ain't got no special powers, other than super gassiness! Everyone's laughing at us now!"

"Sorry, Brute. Not sure what happened," replied Max, releasing more toxic tensions.

The nurse sent them back home on the school's historic horsebus, and told them not to return until they got better.

During the next few days, no one had seen or heard from the bullies, and no one was complaining about it either.

Sammy was sure glad he didn't have any more magic beans. He learned that accepting food from strangers was never a good idea, and relying on unnatural energy was even worse. He told his parents everything that had happened. He mentioned he would still help people, but just not accept anything in return. His parents were proud to hear he had learned a valuable lesson.

IX. Cloaking Cap

Mr. Flynn was relaxing on his chair and leisurely reading through the weekend newspaper when he came across an article that he thought Sammy would like to read.

"Hey, Sammy, I found an interesting article about a senior physicist, Dr. Edward Trotten. It says he was working on this ultra-top secret project for the Department of Defense. Apparently, he vanished before completing his work."

"Hmm... I wonder what happened to him. Can I read it?"

"Sure, here you go."

Sammy was very interested in physics and learned

that Dr. Trotten was last seen in a city ten miles from Old Greenwich. The article went on to mention that he was researching stealth technology. Sammy's concentration broke from loud clanking sounds. "Uh, *helllooo...* Why do you have to make so much noise? I'm trying to read," he said, annoyed.

It was Wendy's turn this weekend to wash dishes. "Sorry, but I gotta finish my chores so we go can go outside."

Sammy was looking forward to exploring in the woods, so he did his best to finish reading the article.

Once they were ready, Wendy grabbed her water bottle and Sammy packed a fruit bar. They rushed out the door.

"Let's race to the lake!" he challenged. They ran along a path, ducking under tree limbs and jumping over fallen branches. Wendy reached the edge of the lake first. They were both of out of breath.

She glanced across the fresh water lake. "Want to explore the old caves?" she asked, still panting.

"Sure." Sammy was tired but motivated by the thought of possibly finding ancient artifacts there.

They continued their hike to the caves, which had formed along the hillside from millions of years of natural erosion. "Looks like the leaves around that entrance have been disturbed. Let's check it out," he suggested.

They carefully approached the opening. Wendy

heard a muffled, moaning sound coming from inside. "Do you hear that?" she whispered.

"Yeah, it might be a bear trying to hibernate." Sammy slowly followed close behind her.

"There aren't any bears in our woods. *Hellllooo...* Anyone there?" she called out.

Just then a weak voice responded, "Help... Help me... I'm over here."

"It's a man! He sounds hurt. Let's go in," said Wendy.

They both cautiously entered, fumbling towards the injured man lying on the ground. "Are you okay, sir? How did you get here?" she asked, handing the stranger her bottle of water.

"Thank you so much, young lady. My name is Ed. I got hurt trying to escape from some bad guys two days ago."

Sammy was curious. "Bad guys? Who were they and why were they after you?"

"Well, I'm not exactly sure, but I suspect they're trying to steal my invention. I was working in my lab when they captured me. They pushed me into the back of this van and we drove off. Luckily, I had my multi-tool and special cap. I managed to cut the rope around my hands and jumped out while the van was still moving. That's how I got hurt."

"How did you get away?" asked Wendy.

"Well, I put on my special cap and they were no longer able to see me. They tried searching for me, but eventually gave up and left, so I made it to this cave to rest."

Sammy began to wonder about the cap. "How come they couldn't see you anymore?" he asked.

"Well, you see, I'm a physicist. I made a huge breakthrough in stealth technology. My cap can make me invisible. It's a cloaking cap! I have to get my formula back before those bad guys find it," explained Ed.

"Are you that physicist, Dr. Edward Trotten?" asked Sammy.

"Yes, I am! How did you know?"

"I just read an article in the newspaper about you this morning. It said you vanished about ten miles from here. No one knows where you are."

"Oh, I didn't expect to get famous this early. I can't tell anyone where I am because I don't know who to trust anymore."

"We can help you. Where's your formula now?" asked Wendy.

"I left it in my desk drawer at the lab. My lab is on the fifth floor of the building next to the City Science Museum. My invention cannot fall into the wrong hands. It's a matter of national security!" stressed Dr. Trotten.

"We understand. Wendy and I will go there after school tomorrow to retrieve it," boldly said Sammy, feeling like a special agent.

"That is very patriotic of you two. Please be careful because it might be dangerous. If you succeed, you will have done this country a great service."

"How will we get into your lab?" asked Wendy.

"You will need to use my entry badge. The code to is 2-8-9-2. Use this cap so no one sees you," instructed Dr. Trotten, handing it to Sammy. He was proud of his invention.

Sammy couldn't wait to test it, so he immediately put it on and vanished.

Wendy panicked. "Sammy! Where did you go?"

"I'm standing right next to you," he teased, tapping her shoulder. She jumped back. He removed the cap and reappeared.

"That's amazing!" she responded.

"Dr. Trotten, we're two of the best investigators this side of town, so don't worry. We'll bring your formula back. Take my fruit bar for energy," offered Sammy, pulling it out of his pocket.

"We have to go now, but we'll come back tomorrow," said Wendy.

"Thank you both kindly, and best of luck," he said as they both left.

That evening during dinner, Sammy told his father that he and Wendy were working on a school project. "Pa, can you please take us to the science museum tomorrow after school?"

"Oh, sure, it sounds like fun! It'll give me a chance to pick up some long overdue supplies from the hardware store," Mr. Flynn replied.

"Thanks, Pa!" The two siblings completed their homework and prepared for bed.

The next morning, Brute and his pals started causing mischief in the back of the bus. Max showed his buddies how to hollow out their pens to shoot spitballs. Zeek crumbled a small piece of paper and stuck it in his mouth. They blew into the pens, causing spitballs to land everywhere, including the ceiling. One hit Sammy on the back of his head.

"Wendy, I just want to give them a piece of my mind!"

"Hmm... Why don't you teach them a little lesson with the cloaking cap instead?" She winked.

"Great idea!" When no one was looking, Sammy placed the cap on his head and immediately vanished. He quietly got up and walked to the back of the bus. Zeek reloaded and was about to blow air into his pen again when Sammy quickly shifted its direction. The spitball shot out and landed right in Brute's nose.

"Ahhh! Zeeko! Whatchya think you'z doin'?"

yelled Brute.

"Uh, sorry about that, it must have been the bump in the road. Let me get that out of there for you," offered Zeek as he attempted to stick his finger into Brute's nose to pull it out.

Brute smacked his hand. "Keeps your fingers outta my nose! I'll dooze it myself!" he yelled, reaching into his own nose to extract it.

The other kids turned and stared in disgust, thinking Brute was trying to pick his nose. He could hear the kids saying, "*Ewww...*" Embarrassed, he quickly pulled his finger back out and decided to wait until he got to school to find a bathroom.

Sammy returned to his seat and quickly removed the cap, unnoticed. He and Wendy laughed.

"That was hilarious, Sammy!" she said as the bus stopped at their school.

The trio stepped off quickly for once. Brute headed straight to the bathroom to resolve his sticky situation. Everyone else went to class.

During science, Sammy's mind began to wander. He started thinking about other pranks he could do with the cloaking cap.

After class, he decided to go to the bathroom and put the cap on. He vanished again and stealthily walked through the halls and into the cafeteria.

He was really excited that no one could see him.

Brute, Max, and Zeek were standing in the lunch line. It was the perfect opportunity to cause mischief, so he carefully walked up behind them.

Brute was hungry as usual, so he snagged a burger and artfully dropped it into Zeek's backpack.

When Zeek was distracted, Sammy reached in the backpack and pulled the burger back out. He then dropped in a bag of unsavory lima beans that his mama had packed him for lunch.

Brute believed he had successfully swindled the burger, so he just purchased a small pack of crackers to justify being in line.

The troublemakers found a table and sat down. Brute's stomach rumbled even louder. "Yo, Zeeko, hands me over the burger, boy, I'm starved!"

Zeek proudly reached into his backpack and pulled out the small bag and handed it to him.

Brute stuck his hand in and pulled out a handful of lima beans. "Ughh... What's this #@#!? Where's my burger??"

"Huh? Didn't you put it in the bag?" he asked in confusion. Just then, Sammy sneakily placed the burger on Zeek's head.

Zeek moved, and the burger fell on the table.

"Oh yeah, so what's that fallin' off of your heads?"

"I don't know how it got there. Really…" whimpered Zeek.

Brute knocked him on his head. "Looks to me like you'z tryin' to steal my stolen burgers, boy!"

Max could see Ms. Brumbreaker, the cafeteria monitor, heading their way. "Hey, guys, chill. The big lady's heading this way."

Sammy, still invisible, picked up Max's hand and quickly flung his fork full of spaghetti in the direction of the cafeteria monitor. It splattered all over the floor just ahead of her.

Max turned to Brute. "Why'd you make me toss the spaghetti, Brute?" he asked loudly, hoping not to be blamed.

"Whatchya talkin's about? I was busy knocking Zeeks over the head for swiping my stolen burger, so how could I be grabbin's your arms at the same time?" asked Brute, trying to defend his dishonor.

All the kids around their table became hushed as Ms. Brumbreaker stared the boys down like an angry bull. She overheard the words "stolen burgers" and saw the mess on the floor. "Alright, you three, I have had just about enough of your hooligan activities this year! Follow me to the Principal's office - NOW!"

Hungry and annoyed, they had no choice but to follow her. Everyone stared as they walked out with their heads down.

Sammy quickly went back to the bathroom and removed the cap. He returned to the cafeteria to enjoy the rest of his lunch in peace with his friends.

The school day ended, but Sammy knew his real mission was about to begin.

The kids on the bus were happy to know that Brute, Max, and Zeek were stuck in detention again. They all enjoyed the ride back home.

"Hi, Mama, we're home!" yelled Sammy.

"Great. Why don't you both get ready for the museum. Your father will be home any minute," reminded Mrs. Flynn.

Sammy and Wendy quickly washed up and gathered their bags. Sammy put the cloaking cap and Mr. Trotten's badge in his backpack. Their father pulled into the driveway, so they headed out and said bye to their mother.

"Hi, kids! Hop on in!" They jumped into their jalopy of a car. It sure was old, but they loved it. The science museum was only ten miles away, so the drive was not very long.

Mr. Flynn parked the car in front of the museum. "Alright, kiddos, I'm going to head to the hardware store. I'll meet you two back here in exactly one hour. Enjoy your project!"

"Okay. Bye, Pa!" Sammy and Wendy could see the building that Mr. Trotten had described. It was further down the street, next to the museum. They headed over.

It was a regular office building with a huge revolving glass door. They peered through the windows and could see the guard at the front desk.

"Come on, Wendy, we don't have much time. You distract him while I sneak by," instructed Sammy. He put the cap on and vanished.

"Okay, but how should I do that?" she asked, looking around for Sammy.

"I don't really know, but I'm sure you'll think of something," he said.

Wendy suddenly remembered she had to write a paper on security for her English class. It was a great opportunity to ask the guard some questions. "How will I know when you're done?" she asked, trying not to move her lips so that no one would think she was talking to herself.

"I'll tug on your backpack, like this. That will be your signal to walk out. I'll be right behind you, so don't worry."

Sammy slipped by while Wendy walked up to the desk.

"How may I help you, young lady?" asked the guard.

"I have a class assignment on security and was wondering if I can interview you."

"Well, sure. I'm not that busy. Nothing unusual ever happens around here anyway."

Wendy continued to distract him while Sammy inserted Dr. Trotten's entry badge into the elevator.

The guard didn't notice it opening.

Sammy took it up to the fifth floor where Dr. Trotten's personal lab was located. Luckily, no one else was around. He inserted the badge into the reader and entered the code that Dr. Trotten had given him. It worked! He quickly ran inside, closing the door behind him.

Sammy looked around and found the desk. He pulled the top drawer open and grabbed the folder that contained the formula. He put it in his bag, then heard a click at the door. Two workers entered. He quietly moved away from the desk and overheard them talking.

"We have to find that formula. It's worth a lot of money to the right buyer," said one guy to the other.

Sammy realized that they were the spies that Dr. Trotten had warned him about. It was a good thing he was invisible. He quickly noted their employee badges and carefully slipped past them. As soon as they entered the file room, he slowly opened the lab door and quietly exited.

Sammy decided to take the stairs so he wouldn't accidentally bump anyone on the elevator. Once he reached the ground level, he walked up to Wendy and tugged her backpack.

She knew it was time to leave, so she thanked the guard for his time and walked out the front door. Sammy followed.

He removed the cap and they rushed back to the science museum. They looked at a few exhibits before returning to the parking lot to meet their father.

"Did you get what you needed?" asked Mr. Flynn.

"Oh, we sure did," replied Wendy, winking to Sammy as they climbed into their car.

Mr. Flynn was also happy that he finally picked up the supplies he needed. They drove back home.

After having snacks, Sammy and Wendy called the police to report that they had found the physicist in the old caves near the lake. Sammy also provided them with the names of the spies.

"Mama, we're heading out to play!" shouted Wendy. The two of them rushed back to the cave.

When they reached the entrance, Sammy called out, "Dr. Trotten... Dr. Trotten... We're back!"

He was still weak, but happy to see they had safely returned. "Hello, Sammy. Hello, Wendy. I'm really glad to see the both of you."

"Mission accomplished! We have your formula! We also called the police to arrest those spies. An ambulance is on its way. And before I forget, here's your cap. I really had a lot of fun with it," said Sammy, smiling.

"Thank you so much. The cap is yours to keep. It's your reward for the good deed. Also, if either of you decide to pursue a career in science, please come find me. I might just have an interesting job waiting for you."

"Cool! Thanks a lot for the cap! We love science, so we'll definitely contact you," replied Sammy.

"We hope you get better soon," said Wendy. They said their goodbyes and returned home.

That evening, Sammy's parents heard the news on the radio about the physicist who was rescued by two mystery kids. The news reporter stated, "The kids recovered his secret work and landed two spies in jail." Dr. Trotten also congratulated the kids on the air for their courageous acts.

"Oh, that's so brave of those children. Don't you agree, Sammy?" asked Mr. Flynn.

Sammy and Wendy just looked at each other with big smiles. They said good night to their parents and headed up to bed.

X. Interstellar Visit

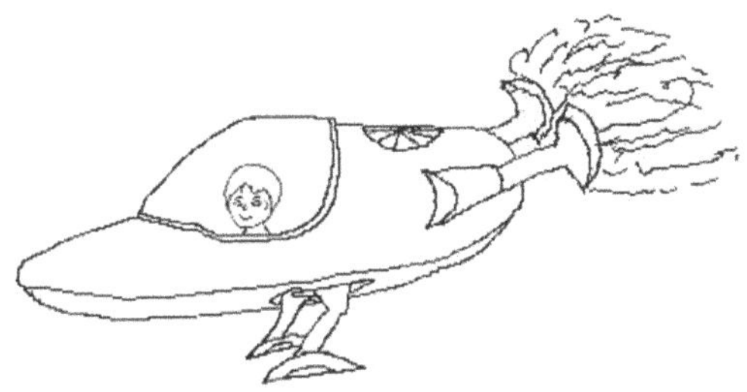

Sammy stayed up late on Saturday night looking at the starry skies with his telescope. "Wendy, come see! The moon looks really interesting up close."

"Okay, but just for a moment," she said, fighting to stay awake. She was sleepy but also curious, so she peered into the eyepiece. "Wow! The moon is really bright. I can even see craters... Wouldn't it be neat if there were planets out there with life like ours?"

Sammy thought about it. "Well, our Milky Way galaxy has over one hundred billion stars and since there are trillions of galaxies across the universe, the 'Drake Equation' shows a *high* possibility that life exists on other planets."

"Drake Equation?"

"Yeah, a scientist, Dr. Frank Drake, created an equation in 1961 as a model to talk about the possibility of life in other parts of our galaxy," explained Sammy.

"Neat. Makes me even more sleepy just thinking about it. Good night," said Wendy as she crawled into the bunk bed.

"Good night." Sammy carefully put away his telescope and lay awake on his sleeping bag, wondering what life would be like in other parts of the universe.

The next morning, they raced down the stairs for breakfast.

"Morning, Mama! Morning, Pa!"

"Good morning, darlings. I made blackberry waffles," Mrs. Flynn said with a smile.

"Awesome! I call syrup!" Wendy reached out and grabbed the bottle first.

After their delicious breakfast, they cleaned their rooms and got ready to head out. Sammy made it down the stairs before Wendy. He could not understand why she took so long getting ready.

She came down and grabbed a water bottle. They put on their shoes and left the house from the back door. They ran through their small yard to reach the woods, the grass still damp from the morning dew.

Sammy noticed a bright reflection near the lake. He shaded his eyes from the sun, squinting at the mysterious object. "Hey Wendy, there's something shiny over there. Let's check it out!"

As they got closer to the edge of the water, they could see an egg-shaped, metallic craft. There was a young boy inside who looked dazed.

Sammy reached for the cockpit's latch and opened it. He could see that the young pilot's outfit had strange, exotic symbols. "Are you okay?" The boy reached out a shaky hand. Sammy helped him out. "Who are you?"

"I'm Vixor," he said, gazing at the siblings with interest. "I was on my very first training flight when these mischievous boys in my squadron knocked me off course."

"Squadron? Aren't you a bit young to be flying, and how did you end up here?" asked Wendy.

"Well, I'm about one hundred and twelve years old-"

"What?! Did you say one hundred and twelve?"

"Yep, I just became eligible for flight training last week," he said proudly.

Sammy and Wendy exchanged surprised looks.

"I'm not exactly sure how I got here. I remember going through a black hole just before falling asleep.

My head probably hit the control panel, sending my craft in this direction. When I awoke, I felt pain, and that's when you two found me. What planet is this anyway? And do you have any water?"

"That's a far out story! You're on Earth in a town called Old Greenwich. Luckily, I do have water. Here ya go." She quickly handed her bottle to him.

"Thanks! Earth? Really? Gosh, I must have traveled pretty far from home." Vixor poured the water into his tank on the topside of the craft.

"Shouldn't you be drinking it instead?" she asked in confusion.

"Well, it's actually fuel for my hydron nebulizer so I can go back home."

"What's a hydron nebulizer?" asked Sammy, peeking into the tank.

"It's a device that fuses hydrogen protons to create high energy. I can use it for gravity wave propulsion and to heal my injuries. Very efficient in my opinion." Vixor stayed connected to it for a few minutes. "See, I'm feeling better already."

"Where exactly are you from?" asked Sammy.

"I'm from a planet called Jambu. Originally, though, my ancestors lived on the planet you now call Mars. Some of the machines they created destroyed the atmosphere, so they had to send a colony to Earth to see if it was habitable. Our colonists were tasked to build outposts on lands you know as India, Egypt, and Peru in order to test their ability to survive. Unfortunately, they could not adapt to Earth's hostile environment due to the ongoing wars between early native populations. They had no choice but to find another planet to live on."

"Then what happened?" asked Wendy, listening intently.

"Well, most of our people abandoned the structures they built on Earth and prepared a temporary colony on your moon. Some of our colonists stayed behind to learn about human culture and languages and to teach our philosophies. They passed their knowledge to us over the centuries using special quantum transmissions through space. And that is how I learned about Earth. The rest of our ancestors searched for a planet suitable for us and found Jambu."

"Where's that?" asked Sammy.

"It's a small planet in the Andromeda galaxy, about two and a half million light years from Earth. Jambu is located in a habitable zone, which is an area of space near a star that can support life. It's very similar to the atmosphere of Mars," explained Vixor.

"Tell us more! What's it like there?" eagerly asked Wendy.

"Well, let me show you." Vixor reached out to hold their hands. He closed his eyes and shared his memories with them.

It was like watching a movie in a planetarium. Jambu was a beautiful planet where people respected nature and focused on living, learning, and loving as their main priorities in life. Although it felt like an hour had passed, it only took a few seconds to experience the flood of images and emotions.

"Wow! That was incredible! I can't believe how simple anti-gravity is on your planet. I never realized that creating a positron vortex would result in the creation of a negative mass field allowing us to rise without residual radiation," commented Sammy.

"We humans have a lot to learn about respecting nature instead of creating pollution, wars, and dangerous weapons. What other powers do you have?" asked Wendy with great curiosity.

"Oh, I wasn't born with any special powers. It's actually my bracelet. Our scientists built them so our people can share information and control objects by thought." The water bottle suddenly floated towards Wendy. Sammy watched in amazement.

She gasped in surprise, catching it. "That's really cool! I wish we had bracelets like that."

Vixor's expression turned serious. "I have to repair my craft to be able to return home. Do you know where I can find some distilled water, graphite, and aluminum?"

"I believe so. Come to school with us tomorrow, and I'm sure we can get what you need. I'll tell my teachers that you're my friend visiting from outside the country. My science teacher, Mr. Beeker, will help us," explained Sammy.

"Great!" Vixor breathed a sigh of relief. "Thanks for your help. I'm grateful to have met both of you."

They quickly covered his spacecraft with leaves and branches to keep it hidden. Vixor followed them back to their house.

"Hi, Mama, we're home, and we brought a friend," Wendy called out.

Mrs. Flynn walked to the door. "How nice. Please come in. What's your name?" she asked.

"I'm Vixor from-"

Sammy interjected, "Uh, he's from outside the country on a student exchange program, and he's going to stay with us tonight. We're going to take him to school tomorrow."

"Well, that sounds great. I hope you enjoy your time with us. Let us know if you need anything, and we'll be having supper soon," responded Mrs. Flynn.

After dinner, the siblings finished their chores and homework and showed Vixor a variety of games. He was very happy to spend time with the Flynns, but also missed being with his own family back home.

The next morning, the three of them prepared for school. Sammy warned Vixor about the bullies as they walked to the bus stop. Luckily, for the next few days, the troublemakers wouldn't be on their bus because they had been assigned elementary school patrol duty as punishment for putting ketchup packets under the bus tires.

"Hey, Jason, this is my friend, Vick. He's visiting from outside the country to learn about our way of life."

"Hey, Vick, nice to meet you. It'll be fun to show you around school today."

"Thanks. I'm happy to be here."

Sammy introduced him to everyone else at the bus stop. They were intrigued by Vixor even without knowing his true origin. The bus ride was enjoyable without the bullies, but Sammy knew they might still run into them at school.

During science class, Sammy asked Mr. Beeker if he and Vixor could conduct an experiment in the woods for extra credit. The teacher was delighted and provided them with the exact items they needed.

Max had been eavesdropping on Sammy earlier and decided to tell Zeek about it. "Yo, Zeek, I just heard Sammy's gonna be doing an experiment after school with his new exchange buddy," he said, leaning against the table.

"Should we be doing some extra credit too?" sincerely asked Zeek.

"No, Zeekster, that's not what I meant! We have to catch up with them in the woods and give them a hand with their experiment. Get what I mean?"

"Uh, yeah, sure, but why are we helping them?"

"Never mind! You'll get the picture later," replied Max, frustrated with Zeek's inability to catch on quickly to his devious idea.

After class, Max told Brute about his plan. The three of them decided that they would head to the woods after patrol duty. Brute was always up for shenanigans. "We'z can runs our own gravity experiments to see what happens when their bottles drops from our hands," the leader snickered.

After school, Sammy, Wendy, and Vixor headed back to his craft near the lake after having some snacks.

Vixor took out his supplies, and used the graphite to repair his electronic circuits. Sammy watched in curiosity. "What are you using that for?" he asked.

"Oh, the graphite becomes a super conductor when it's only one atomic layer thick. I can use it to repair the electronics panel, and I'll use the aluminum to repair the small tear on the nose," he explained.

"So, what's the distilled water for, then?"

"It's a clean source of energy for the nebulizer."

All three of them worked together to repair the craft. "I think it's just about ready," Vixor said.

"Oh, that's great. Do you think you can go home now?" asked Wendy, concerned.

"I hope so. Just a few more tweaks and I'll be set." Just as he said that, sparks flew out of the cockpit's panel. "Um, speaking of which, could you hand me the quantum stabilizer?"

As they continued to work on the craft, the troublemakers were lurking in the woods looking for them.

"Hey, Brute, I see them over there, near the lake. What's that strange, shiny thing next to them?" asked Max, eyes focusing.

"Yeah, I seez them. Let's head over there to finds out," responded Brute. The three of them made their way towards the lake and popped out from behind the trees.

"Yo, Sammy, we heard you're doing some extra credit for Mr. Beeker. Anything to do with this strange machine?" asked Max, pretending to be friendly. The gang peered at the craft in curiosity.

"Uh, what are you three doing out here? Aren't you supposed to be doing kiddie patrol?" asked Sammy.

"We'z finished that and wanted to hangs out down here at the lake. You'z got a problems with that?" Brute casually asked, clenching his fists.

Zeek jumped into the conversation. "We thought we'd help you out with your gravity experiment."

"Gravity experiment? Who told you that?" asked Sammy.

Brute knocked Zeek on the head. "Yo, Zeeko, didn't I tell you'z to leave the education stuffs to me and Max here?" he scolded.

"Oh, sure, Brute, I thought we were going to drop some-"

Max interrupted. "Never seen a machine like this before. And that bracelet your friend is wearing looks pretty neat. Tell him to hand it over!"

Vixor didn't want trouble for Sammy or Wendy, so he quickly removed it and handed it to him.

"Max, don't fool around with that bracelet. You need to give it back to him right now!" demanded Wendy.

Max ignored her and slipped it on his hand. While poking at it, his mind began to wander, and the craft began to power up. "Hey, guys, did you see that? Let's get in." The three of them crawled into the cockpit and squeezed together to share the seat.

"Yo, Max, why is the tops closin' down on us?" nervously asked Brute.

"Uh, I don't know," he shrugged, thinking hard as the craft began to rise.

Sammy turned to Vixor, "They're always causing trouble, and they don't know what they're doing. You have to stop them!" he anxiously requested.

"My ship is set to automatically return home. I can't stop them without my bracelet."

As the craft began to rise even faster, the trio had a sudden change of mind.

"Max! Get us back down, I think I'm getting sea sick," shouted Zeek.

"We're in the air, not on the sea! And I'm not sure how to get us down. Get your belts on! We're going really high!" yelled Max.

"It's beginning to get darks around us!" exclaimed Brute.

"Yeah, that's because we're in outer space! Sorry, guys. If we make it back alive, I promise to be good for a month!" cried Max.

The craft accelerated to near light speed. They caught a glimpse of the moon and other planets as they whizzed by. They were flying towards the center of the Milky Way galaxy.

"Say, what's that huge dark spots in the middle there?" asked Brute with even more concern.

"Don't look now, but I think we're heading into a black hole! It's been great knowing you guys," said Max, believing it would be his last words.

As the craft crossed the event horizon, they felt an immense force pulling them down. Everything became blurry and they instantly fell into a deep sleep.

After a brief moment, the craft came out of the black hole, and with a sudden jerk, it emerged into an unknown part of space.

They felt groggy coming out of their sleep. As their eyes opened, they thought they were peering into a huge mirror. There was another identical craft in front of them, except the three boys in it looked even naughtier than they did.

The unfamiliar boys on the other craft stared back at them. "Hey, isn't that Vixor's craft? I don't see him in there. And who are those strange looking boys in it?" asked Qyven.

"I've never seen them before. Maybe Vixor is hiding in the trunk," suggested Dufra.

Balster knocked Dufra on his head. "How many times do I have to tell you it's a spacecraft, not a car!"

"Whoever they are, they sure look like sitting ducks. Let's blast them for more points on our training record!" shouted Qyven. He pressed a button on their weapon's panel. It released a sudden burst of light that enveloped Vixor's craft. It was some sort of low-powered electrostatic ray that energized the cockpit.

The glare blinded Brute, Max, and Zeek for a moment. Zeek fumbled around for a sunshade, but he accidentally hit the reverser instead, sending them back into the black hole.

"Oh, not again...," groaned Brute as their craft swiftly accelerated backward. Almost immediately, they fell asleep again. The craft took them all the way back to the lake.

Vixor and the siblings were surprised to see that the craft had returned. Vixor opened the cockpit hatch, quickly taking his bracelet back while the boys were still asleep. Using it, he lifted the trio into the air and carefully placed them under a tree.

"Thank goodness my craft is still operational. I better head back before these boys wake up." He jumped into the pilot's seat and saluted Sammy and Wendy. "Thank you so much for your help. I will miss you both. Maybe someday I can come back to visit."

"We'll miss you too. And if you run into those bullies on your side again, don't let them push you around," advised Sammy.

Vixor winked as the cockpit door closed over him. He waved goodbye. Sammy and Wendy waved back as he flew away.

"Let's leave those boys here to work off their nap," suggested Wendy. They rushed back home.

Vixor traveled back through the black hole to his galaxy. After successfully out-maneuvering the three bullies in his squadron with his modified propulsion unit, Vixor managed to safely return to his base on the planet Jambu.

Back on Earth, Brute, Max, and Zeek began to wake up, yawning and stretching their arms.

Not remembering why he was lying under a tree,

Zeek was the first to speak. "Guys, I had the worst dream. We were flushed down this black hole and got zapped by three funny looking aliens with a ray gun!"

Finally managing to focus his eyes, Brute stared at the other two. With a sudden shock and burst of memory, he shouted, "Ahhh! &*#@! Wasn't no dreams, check outs our hairs! It's stickin' ups all over the place!"

The static charge from the ray burst created a wonderful hair-do for them. The gang knew that no one would believe their story, so they returned to school embarrassed with their new hairstyles.

Max kept his promise to be good for a month and didn't bother any of the other kids. Brute and Zeek on the other hand, just waited for their hair to go back to normal before stirring up more trouble again...

ABOUT THE AUTHOR

R.K. Bandi, born in the United States, was brought up in Georgia, New Jersey, and Virginia. He particularly enjoyed growing up in the 70's, 80's, and 90's. He is first and foremost a philosopher at heart with a simple belief that living, learning, and loving is all that is needed to experience the best that life has to offer. He is also an entrepreneur and computer scientist, but believes that nature is of higher importance than technology. R.K. Bandi has had the pleasure of experiencing multiple points of view in religion, science, and cultures of the world. His inspiration for writing this book came from telling nightly tales of adventure with twists of humor, science fiction, and fantasy to his three beautiful children in order to impart knowledge and ignite their imagination. His stories convey the importance of positive relationships between family and friends, and the unique and hilarious ways to deal with spectacular challenges.

Lightning Source UK Ltd.
Milton Keynes UK
UKHW01n1935260618
324837UK00001B/1/P

9 781732 073906